Ryan felt the pressure of someone's touch on his chest, the contact light and tentative. His eyes snapped open and he clamped his hand around the woman's wrist. She jumped and tugged in a vain effort to retrieve her captured hand.

She could have shot him.

She could have left the car and made a run for it.

But she'd decided to check his condition instead. It wasn't wise. But it was kind. How long since he'd seen this sort of compassion?

"Haley," he whispered. "What happened?"

"You fainted, I think."

"Passed out," he said and stretched his back until his neck pressed to the headrest. "Marines don't faint."

"Is that what you are now? A marine? Not a detective?"

He blew out a breath. "Once a marine..."

She lifted her chin and gave him an appraising stare with those bright, intelligent eyes.

"Look, if I tell you the truth, chances are good you won't believe me. But if you are captured, you'll know that you died protecting your country."

DEFENSIVE ACTION

JENNA KERNAN

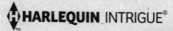

For Jim, always.

ISBN-13: 978-1-335-60449-1

Defensive Action

Copyright © 2019 by Jeannette H. Monaco

Recycling programs for this product may not exist in your area.

Printed in U.S.A.

Jenna Kernan has penned over two dozen novels and received two RITA® Award nominations. Jenna is every bit as adventurous as her heroines. Her hobbies include recreational gold prospecting, scuba diving and gem hunting. Jenna grew up in the Catskills and currently lives in the Hudson Valley in New York State with her husband. Follow Jenna on Twitter, @jennakernan, on Facebook or at jennakernan.com.

Books by Jenna Kernan

Visit the Author Profile page at Harlequin.com.

CAST OF CHARACTERS

Ryan Carr—CIA operative responsible for the collection and delivery of vital intelligence on a looming terrorist attack. He will stop at nothing to complete his assignment.

Haley Nobel—A risk-averse urban professional who wants only to survive the mess in which she has become entangled.

Takashi Watanabe—A foreign operative and Ryan's contact.

Siming's Army—A foreign terrorist organization orchestrating a doomsday attack on the USA.

Hornet, Needle and Fin—Assassins hired to kill Ryan and recover the intelligence he carries.

Colonel Jorge L. Hernandez—Ryan's former commanding officer and longtime confidant.

Colonel Charles Braiser—Colonel Hernandez's representative.

Chapter One

"Turn around or keep going?" Haley Nobel muttered to the car's empty interior. There was no one in the rental with her to answer and she realized it was the first time she had been outside alone, all alone, in years.

The GPS app had taken a holiday during her drive in the Adirondack Mountains of New York State and the darkness had fallen like a curtain outside her shadow-blue 2018 Ford Taurus. Beyond the windshield there were no twinkling stars. No bright moon. No mystical glimmer of the aurora borealis. Just blackness with the only sign of life being the deer that had darted across the road a few miles back and nearly given her a heart attack.

Adult adventure camp was looking increasingly like the colossal mistake she'd expected it to be. She had about as much business being back here as that deer would have on the Number 7 Subway.

"Where am I?" she asked the silence about her as she peered at the gas gauge that had dipped below a quarter-tank of fuel.

She shivered against the chill, trying again to adjust

to the heat on a night that was forecast to dip into the thirties. She'd forgotten that summer nights were so much colder up here in the mountains.

Her light L.L.Bean jacket looked rugged in the catalog but it was designed for wind and rain, not cold. There wasn't even a fleece liner. Inside one of the front pockets was her impulse buy, offered at checkout for 25 percent off, a Victorinox Rambler pocketknife including scissors, file, two screwdrivers, bottle opener, toothpick, wire-stripper, tweezers, key ring and a blade long enough to use to slit her own throat for being stupid enough to let her father convince her to leave her upstairs apartment in the building she owned in Williamsburg, Brooklyn, to redeem his Hanukkah gift to her.

She'd been planning the specifics of this week for six months and it was already here. Back in December, she'd thought her father had a point. She did need to get back out there. But rocketing down zip lines was a little too out there. Besides, her job furnished all the thrills and chills she needed, strictly virtual, of course.

She'd tried to get him to take the gift back but he'd said it was nonrefundable and then told her that she needed to stop acting like she was the one who had died.

That cut deep, but the more she thought about it, the more she felt he might be right. But perhaps going out with friends for drinks would have been a better start than kayaking in white water.

Haley had told her father that her life held plenty of risks, which wasn't exactly true. Hacking wasn't dangerous if you were paid by the company you were hacking, which she always was. Her father thought she was paid by local businesses to build websites and manage social media accounts.

Her dad also thought she sat alone in her room all day taking customer service calls and playing video games. The video games part was true. But she had adventures in the real world. She'd recently gotten highlights in her light brown hair, which no one noticed as the color she picked was so close to her original shade.

You're not the one who died, Haley.

As if she could just flip a switch and make herself like she had been, bring her sister back and go on bumbling along doing stupid stuff as if there would never be any consequences for either of them. She could not go back to that girl, not after losing Maggie. And if that were even possible, it would definitely take longer than one week. But when it came to telling her father she was not going, she just couldn't do it. Maybe she could stay in a hotel near the camp, take a few photos and send them home. Snagging a video of one of the other female campers as she careened down the zip line would be good, too.

Except yesterday dad had pointed out that the camp was technology-free. How had she missed that nugget on the web page?

Maybe her dad was right about her having lost her joy. Was joy tied to doing stupid things, like jumping off a forty-foot cliff into freezing cold lake water?

What was even the point of that anyway?

If anything happened to you, too, it would just kill me. Her mother's words played in her head along with the declaration that no mother should have to live to see the death of a child—until she had.

Haley blew out a breath. When had she started sweating?

If anything happened to you, too...you two...

Dad wanted her back out there. She saw the gift for what it was: a Hail Mary pass, a last-ditch effort to remind her of what she'd put aside. Meanwhile, Mom sent Haley links to articles on tick bites and how to recognize poisonous snakes.

What was she doing? Rock climbing...hiking...canoeing? Bouldering...which, judging from the website photo, was just risking a fall from an unreasonable height onto a bed of broken shards of jagged rock. She was no longer the adventurous one. Not since losing Maggie made her the only one.

What got her into the rental car in the first place was the thought of having to hide out all week in hopes that no one would notice she had not gone through with it. Having told her coworkers that she'd be offline and in the mountains, it was now impossible to back out without everyone knowing she had done so.

Whose stupid advice was it to declare your intentions publicly?

Oh, right, her dad's again.

And she somehow felt that working out at her gym and hiking from Midtown to Lower Manhattan failed to prepare her for hiking along ledges while carrying a pack that would make a Sherpa blanch.

The photos of happy, healthy tanned hikers on the singles outing had gotten stuck in her head. She had forgotten the only bugs she managed were virtual and she'd never had a tan in her entire life. Her skin was so white that, under fluorescent lighting, it looked blue.

She peered ahead. Were those taillights? She exhaled her relief.

She glided closer to the other vehicle. It was a biggish car, like a Cadillac or Mercedes sedan. The plates were from Ontario.

"Oh, great. They're probably as lost as I am."

The sedan's brake lights flashed as it slowed at the sharp turn, clearly identified by the road sign of an arrow bent at a ninety-degree angle accompanied by the reduced-speed-warning sign. They'd pulled ahead as she prepared early to make the turn.

Then the side door behind the driver of the sedan flew open and she moved her hand to her horn to alert the driver.

Something tumbled out onto the road. At first she thought it was one of those army duffel bags, the really big ones. But then she realized it was something wrapped in an olive green blanket, rolling along the road. She slammed on her brakes as her mind registered a human form and blood on a pale face.

Haley yelped as she judged the distance between the figure on the road and her decelerating auto. Too short, she realized and turned the wheel, swerving and squeezing her eyes shut tight. She braced against the wheel and lifted her shoulders to her ears. Her sharp inhalation merged with the sound of her phone tumbling from the cup holder and into the wheel well at her feet. The Taurus shuddered to a halt as the antilock brakes engaged. There had been no thump of tires rolling over a body.

She opened her eyes. The car ahead of her continued on, seemingly oblivious.

The cones of her headlights showed nothing but dry empty pavement. Had she imagined it?

Something thumped against her driver's door. Haley yelped and glanced out the side window into the face of a man lying on his back inside a blanket that had been secured like a rug with clear tape around his torso and legs.

"Jeepers!" she croaked and opened the door, which thumped against the man's hiking boots.

The cab light illuminated a rectangle of pavement on which the man lay. He sat up, struggling with the blanket until he released the tape, compromised in his roll. Then he held up his hands, bound together with silver-gray tape. Duct tape, she realized, the kind her dad had in his tool kit. The blanket fell away from him, revealing his shirtless torso streaked with sweat, grime and blood.

Her eyes bulged. Deep brown eyes glittered above the strip of silver duct tape that covered his mouth. For just an instant she thought she might be part of some elaborate practical joke, some "gotcha" reality TV program. But the blood was real and so were the abrasions. He lifted his bound wrists again, insisting.

"Yes," she said and placed the car in Park before spinning in her seat, leaving the car running. What was she doing?

He was in danger…so *she* was in danger.

Her new jacket flopped open and something heavy bounced against her hip. The Rambler pocketknife with ten tools, she realized, one of which was a knife blade.

She scrambled to kneel at his side and fumbled with the pocketknife, dropping it on the road. When she retrieved it, her hands were shaking so badly, she could not get her thumbnail into the slot designed to be used to retract the blade.

He was sitting up now, blood streaming from a cut above his eye as he extended his bound hands, silently asking for the knife.

"I can do it," she said. "I practiced."

His hands jerked out, adamant.

She deferred. "Fine."

She place the multi-tool in his cupped palms. He flipped the knife about, flicked open the blade and then tossed the open knife in the air, catching it so that the blade was now up and pointing back toward the tape that secured his wrists. Then he neatly sliced through his bonds.

Haley tottered back on her rump at this display of… what, exactly? Pocketknife proficiency. Who was this guy?

An instant later, he had the tape off his mouth and had ahold of her upper arm in a grip that said he was both strong and dangerous.

"Get in," he said and shoved her toward the car.

Oh, no way, she thought.

She heard the sound of tires screeching and glanced up to see red brake lights flare on the big shiny sedan now making an illegal U-turn on the double solid. Head-lights now blinded her.

They're coming back!

What was the greater risk? she wondered, trying vainly to analyze the situation as her heart sped with the wheels of the approaching auto.

"What's happening?" she shouted, hardly recognizing her voice because it was a full octave higher than usual.

Broad hands grabbed her rump and shoved, sending her sprawling across the console and into the passenger seat of her rental.

She was still facedown on the upholstery when he slid under her legs and into the driver's seat.

"Move!" he shouted at her.

Instantly, she crumpled herself into a ball and contorted herself like a magician's assistant until she was kneeling backward on the passenger seat.

"What are you doing?" she yelled as he threw the car into Drive.

The momentum caused by his foot slamming down on the accelerator forced her face into the headrest. A moment later, she spun in place and dropped into the bucket seat.

She aimed a finger at him. "This is my car!"

Technically it was a rental, but it sure was her credit card and her signature on the line that said she wanted to buy the optional liability coverage and damage protection, which was voided if she was not the only driver.

He didn't look at her and a moment later she saw why. They were rocketing through the night at the sedan that sped toward them. It was like a joust at the yearly Renaissance Faire, except instead of horses and wooden lances, these contestants were using two-ton automobiles. Their opponent was riding the modern-day equivalent of a warhorse and they were astride a borrowed mule.

"Look out!" she hollered, as if he could have missed the oncoming vehicle.

"Seat belt," he said through gritted teeth.

She understood and panic flashed cold on her skin. He was going to crash them on purpose.

Haley drew the belt across herself with trembling hands and somehow clicked it home. She pressed back into the seat as if the inches she gained would somehow protect her. She glanced at the airbag warning on the dash, afraid she was going to feel the impact first-hand. Her gaze flicked back to the oncoming sedan and she thought she saw someone leaning out the window behind the driver.

The stranger beside her grasped her by the neck and forced her head down as if readying her for crash position aboard a doomed 747. She bit her lip and tasted blood as her upper teeth sliced through it. There was a sound like glass breaking and then a cracking noise that reminded her of the sound the ice in an ice-cube tray made when you twisted it. Bits of glass rained down upon her.

He draped his body over hers as the side window exploded.

Someone was shooting at them!

"Who's driving?" she yelled, knowing he couldn't simultaneously drive and lie across her like a fire blanket.

He straightened and she did the same. The window before her was now a mosaic of tiny squares of glass. Wind whistled through four holes in the middle of each circular epicenter of disaster. But the sedan was gone.

She pressed a hand to her heart, feeling it jackhammer. Turning in her seat, she saw that the driver's window had folded in half, as if cleaved by an ax. Her side mirror dangled from a series of wires and the sedan was behind them on the shoulder.

"Ha. Ha!" she crowed, pointing. "They're stuck!"

Her hysterical elation ebbed as the sedan's red taillights flared. The vehicle moved back onto the road and turned.

When she next spoke, she was surprised at the deadpan quality of her voice.

"They're following us."

Chapter Two

Haley glanced back to the highway and the guardrail that cascaded past her window at dizzying speeds. Then she turned to the shirtless stranger, who was dressed in pants streaked with grease. Blood oozed from the road rash on his shoulder and she wondered if he was staining the upholstery.

The ridiculousness of that worry forced a hysterical laugh from Haley. He glanced from the road to her and she covered her mouth to block out the worrisome sound of her panic-stricken giggle.

He was clean-shaven with dark brown hair cut short enough for her to see the gash on his scalp above his ear. His sooty lashes framed deep brown eyes that took her breath away.

"You okay?" he asked, scanning her with those arresting eyes.

"I don't think so." She pointed to the blood that trickled down his forehead. "You're bleeding."

His biceps flexed and his pecs strained as he turned the wheel. Haley's ears buzzed, from fear, she told herself, but the tingling awareness that made her skin pucker was something else altogether.

He had glanced at her for only an instant, yet she was breathless. His attention now on the road, she forced herself to look away from his athletic figure and the skin that glowed a healthy golden-bronze. Her attention landed on the speedometer. Was he going ninety miles an hour on this crummy, poorly maintained stretch of lonely highway?

They spoke in unison.

"That's too fast," she said, pointing at the dash.

"Thanks for stopping," he said, glancing to the rearview mirror. "Do you have something to clear away this glass?"

Only then did Haley glance forward. How could he even see? The front windshield was a web of tiny bits of shatter-resistant glass held together by some clear film.

"I don't know. Golf umbrella?" She'd gotten it free when opening a bank account despite the fact that she did not golf and that it was miles too big for use on a city street. She had lots of bank accounts now, all over town.

"Great." He held out his hand. Duct tape still clung to the dark hairs on his forearm.

She scrambled in the seat behind her, past the bags of groceries to the umbrella wedged beneath.

"Is that food?" he asked.

"Yes." As if she'd travel four to six hours without food, a first-aid kit and a mobile-phone charger.

"Do you have anything to drink?"

She thought of the thermos half full of cold coffee and instead opted for something unopened. A moment later, she returned her backside to the seat holding the golf umbrella in one hand and a bottle of Snapple Grapeade in the other.

He grasped the umbrella first in one hand and used the handle to pound. His muscles corded and relaxed again and again until he'd punched a hole the size of a basketball from the windshield before him. Now wind whistled through the cab.

She held out the Snapple. He lay the umbrella between the seats and took the bottle, holding it for her to open.

Haley tried one-handed, but of course couldn't make the cap come loose. So she gripped his hand with hers and twisted, feeling immediately sorry because the heat of his hand and the long elegance of his cupped fingers made her insides tighten. The cap popped.

The stranger brought the bottle to his lips and drank, draining the contents in three long swallows. Haley blinked in astonishment. Liquid clung to his lips and a droplet trickled over the shadow of a beard. He captured the escaping fluid with his pink tongue.

A flame of unwanted desire flashed to life inside her. Haley swallowed hard and sat back in her seat clutching one arm around her quivering stomach.

"Would you please tell me what is happening?" Had she just said please to the man who had hijacked her and her car? She squeezed her eyes shut. She had.

"Kidnapped," he said.

Her hands went to her mouth. Her mother's fears coming true. She was being abducted. "Oh, my goodness."

"Not you. Me."

She nodded, unable to speak.

"I'm an undercover detective and those guys are the ones I'm investigating. They made me. Now they're bringing me out here to kill me and dump my body. That's after they tortured me to find out what we know. Said they'd tear my teeth out one by one with a pair of pliers."

Her skin went clammy. She glanced behind them. They were being pursued by mobsters.

"You have a phone?" he asked.

She pointed to the wheel well at his feet. "No reception."

He made a scoop and captured the mobile, checking for a signal and then dropping the useless thing into the cup holder.

"What's your name?"

"Haley Nobel."

"Well, Haley, I'm Detective Howard Insbrook."

What did she say now? Certainly not a pleasure because this was anything but.

"Nice to… Hi."

He cast her an odd look.

"Where you from?" he asked.

"Born in Albany, NY, now living in Brooklyn." She answered as if under investigation.

"I work on a joint task force on organized crime out of Glens Falls," he said. "What is it you do?"

She hesitated. "Uh, I'm a computer programmer."

"Who for?"

"Independent. I take on contract work, here and there. Work from home. You know."

Her latest gig was an important client, the US Department of Homeland Security, but she wasn't telling him that. She had a clearance level and everything. Unfortunately the job included not telling friends and family exactly what she was up to.

"Hmm," he said and his gazed flicked to the rearview.

The sedan was just behind them. He swerved and braked, causing the other vehicle to appear to rocket up beside them. She glimpsed the passenger clearly through the collapsed window. He was pointing a handgun at them but their pursuers zipped forward until Haley's front fender came parallel with the mobster's rear door.

Detective Insbrook turned hard into the side of the opposite car as he punched the gas.

She pressed both palms to the ceiling upholstery and screamed but the sound was lost over the shriek of metal raking over metal.

The sedan turned before her rental car, pushed into an involuntary spin that sent the opposite vehicle careening by her passenger-side window and into the guardrail as they whizzed on.

"Where did you learn to do that?"

"The academy," he said.

She craned her neck to see the pursuit vehicle piled against the guardrail, the hood crumpled like a crushed aluminum can.

They wouldn't be able to see over that hood, even if the car was drivable. She turned back to him.

"I don't think they can come after us now," she said.

"But they will. And soon."

The relief sizzled away like fat dropped on a skillet and she pressed herself back into the seat. Her stomach hurt.

He drove with one hand now, and she saw the other was black and blue, as if someone had beaten him with a stick or a pipe or a sock with a roll of quarters or one of those...

Her phone chirped as it came back online.

"Rerouting," said her phone's navigation program. She snatched it up and saw she still had no service, but the GPS system was working.

"Huh. We're only five miles from the camp," she said. She had been heading in the right direction after all.

"You own a place up here?"

"No." She stared at her phone. "I'm enrolled in adventure camp for a week."

She glanced from the screen to him. He squinted at her, as if trying to determine if she was kidding.

Her dad thought the wilderness experience would stir her emotions and bring back the girl he had known, but that girl was gone. Dead gone.

"We can't go there," he said.

"Why not?"

"They have your plates."

"It's not my car. I rented it."

"Doesn't matter. These men can trace it to you."

Fear filled her belly like chips of ice. If her work hacking systems taught her anything, it was how ridiculously easy it was to gain useful information.

His gaze flashed to the rearview and his jaw clenched, making the muscles there bulge. She knew what he saw. A turn of her head confirmed her fear. Behind them was a pair of halogen headlights.

"Is that them?"

He inclined his head and scowled at the road ahead.

"They're gaining," she said.

"Four cylinders," he grumbled.

She'd been offered an upgrade but she'd turned it down.

The lights blinded her, illuminating the cab as the sedan closed the distance between them. The impact of the sedan slamming into their bumper sent Haley heaving forward. She was prevented from striking the dashboard by the cinching of her shoulder restraint. The Taurus skidded off the road, pushed by the sedan. Headlights skittered over a wall of pine-tree trunks. She had one instant to hold her breath and close her eyes before impact. The metal pounded the solid wood, collapsing as both front and side airbags exploded against her.

Chapter Three

Haley blinked her eyes open. Everything was white. She punched at the inflated airbag that gradually deflated. A fine dust swirled about the cabin, bright as chalk dust in the glow of the overhead cab light. She turned her head toward the driver's seat and her neck gave a sharp pang.

"Ouch," she whispered to no one. She blinked at the empty seat beside her and the open door. Where was Detective Insbrook?

She couldn't open her door. Finally, she unfastened her safety belt and wiggled across the console to the driver's seat. For once it was an advantage to be only five feet tall.

Haley pressed the starter button but heard only a click. The smell of gasoline aroused her dulled senses. She had to get out of the vehicle. She planted one foot on the floor mat and it rolled off something metallic. Glancing down she found her thermos. She gathered it up and then thought to collect her purse. Her mobile phone was no longer connected to the charger and her initial search yielded nothing. That was when she heard the first gunshot.

She hunched and half fell, half crawled out of the compartment, landing on hands and knees. The wet loam of pine needles immediately soaked the denim of her jeans and the ground felt soft and prickly, all at once. She scented moist earth and pine. Her voluminous purse fell forward, sliding under her chest and dragging on the ground before her.

What was happening?

She saw him then, the detective, crouching at the front fender holding her golf umbrella in two fists like a batter waiting for a pitch. Into her view stepped a pair of legs draped in cuffed trousers. The person wore the sort of expensive lace-up leather shoes she associated with Wall Street types and politicians. The fine brown leather was never intended for this sort of terrain.

She glimpsed the bottom of a dark wool overcoat and then Insbrook straightened and swung the umbrella. The blow hit the man's arm as he fired a shot into the side of the Ford near Haley's head. As the two locked together and grappled for the weapon, Haley scuttled on all fours in the opposite direction.

From behind the tangle of pine and crumpled front fender came the men grunting, coupled with the thud of them falling against the mangled auto and then the ground. She pressed her hands to her ears and then realized she still had her index finger looped in the handle of the cup fixed to the top of the metal thermos. A quick glance back showed her that the detective held her knife in a hand clasped by his attacker, who held a pistol in a hand captured by the detective. What neither of them saw was the third man, who made his way forward from the sedan to stand behind the wrestling pair with a raised handgun. He was similarly dressed to Insbrook's opponent, had light brown skin and seemed to be waiting until he could get a clean shot at the detective, currently on his back on the ground. He sidestepped the grappling pair until he stood just beyond the pine tree where she crouched.

Haley's heart seemed to have moved to her throat and each beat ached. She pressed herself to the tree trunk, using its solid support to help her rise. Then she weighed her options. If the second man turned now, he'd shoot her dead. She glanced to the forest. She could just run into the woods. Find a place to hide. He might hear her and come after her. That thought made her throat ache even worse. Could she hide in the darkness until the men were dead or gone?

She closed her eyes as she fought against the urge to help Insbrook.

Don't be stupid. You're not a cop. You've never even seen a gun.

But they were going to kill him. She knew it in her heart. They would shoot him down and then they would find her. What if he had a family, children? What would happen to her mom if she lost her only surviving child?

Haley drew in a deep breath and clamped her jaw tight. Her sister had fought for her life. Haley would do the same.

She gripped the thermos in two sweating hands and crept along the opposite side of the rear bumper, inching toward the tall brown-skinned man still trying for a shot at the detective.

The metal exterior of the thermos felt cold in her hand as she hoisted it high. She had a moment's hesitation as she stared at the stubble of his shaved head and the large shiny patch at the crown where hair no longer grew. It was enough time for the man to sense her there. He turned his head. She was out of time. Haley rose up on her tiptoes and swung. Her right hand clutched the thermos and her left gripped her opposite wrist. The sound at contact and the reverberation hit her simultaneously. Blood spurted from the gash she created in his scalp with the bottom edge of the bludgeon.

"Oh, gosh!" she said as the man completed his turn and sank to one knee. He used his free hand to reach up to the top of his head and pressed it over the wound. Then he drew it away and stared silently at the blood that smeared his palm. He never looked at her. The gun dropped from his hand and she snatched it up by the barrel.

She glanced toward the detective to find he had his legs wrapped around his opponent's neck and held one of his own ankles to increase the force of the choke hold. The man gasped and struggled, his purple face illuminated in terrifying color by the cab light.

Haley staggered back two steps as the man went limp.

"Get their keys," said the detective.

She shook her head and continued to look between the bleeding man, now on hands and knees, and the big one who lay motionless beside the car.

"Is he…?"

"Choked out. Now hurry." The detective was already

searching his opponent, coming up with a wallet but no keys.

The amount of blood issuing from the head wound she had caused made her queasy. But she tucked the thermos under her arm, crept forward and used her free hand to reach into one of the large side pockets. She felt a wallet and reached past in search of the keys but found nothing. Withdrawing her hand, the wallet fell to the ground and flopped open. The badge and ID were unmistakable. DEA was printed in large blue letters and the gold shield looked very official. Not a wallet, she realized. It was the identification of a representative from the Drug Enforcement Agency of the United States. And she had just clobbered him over the head and taken his gun.

She gaped up at the detective, if he were a detective.

"Let's go." He grabbed her arm and hustled them toward the agents' car.

She pulled back and shook her head. What if they were trying to apprehend a criminal and she'd brained one of them?

"There's one more," he said, pressing her down behind the front of the car. "Wait here." He pointed at the ground and, as if she were his hound, she sank to her knees.

He gripped his enemy's gun and disappeared from her sight.

Haley heard the sedan door chime and then gunfire. Four rapid discharges. *Pop-pop-pop-pop*, like a string of firecrackers. Then came a thud.

She bit down on her fist and waited.

Run, you idiot.

But her legs would not lift her and her knees clanked together like the Tin Man's in *The Wizard of Oz*.

"Come up," he called.

Haley lowered her hand and rose. Then she ran in the opposite direction toward the woods. He had her around the waist before she reached the beckoning darkness of the tree line. He hauled her off her feet. One iron arm gripped her about the waist.

He ignored her struggles as he carried her past the two still figures. A third lay beside the open passenger door that now held four bullet holes. The driver lay facedown, red head turned to the side. One eye stared vacantly out and his mouth gaped. There were four holes in the back of his jacket.

The door chime had ceased and all she could hear was the blood pounding in her eardrums.

"Is he…?"

"Get in," he ordered and set her on her feet.

She took a step away from him. He captured her wrist, the one holding the bloody thermos. There could be no mistake now. He'd killed this man. Detectives did not shoot people down and then run.

"I don't have time to argue." He opened the passenger door and shoved her inside. It was then she realized she had the DEA officer's gun, but was still holding it upside down.

When he got into the driver's side, she had it the right way around, at her side between the passenger-side door and the bucket seat. She was no longer defenseless.

Haley found herself inside the stolen sedan as they

rocketed backward onto the road. The man she had brained with the thermos was now standing. He hunched with one hand on the trunk and the other holding his gashed head, illuminated in a perfect still image in the sweep of the headlights before they raced past the pair.

She'd seen the badge of the DEA agent and she was fairly certain the ID was a counterfeit. She cast a glance at the bleeding, dirty man who had represented himself as a detective. Her gut told her that had also been a lie. So did she challenge this stranger or keep quiet?

He'd forced her into this car and what had started as an act of mercy on her part now seemed a mistake so grand that adventure camp paled in comparison.

This was a kidnapping—her kidnapping.

She looked down at her hands, one holding the thermos and the other gripping the agent's gun.

RYAN CARR CLENCHED the wheel and headed down the open road. He'd taken these goons on a wild-goose chase, ending with him rolling out of a car moving way faster than he'd realized. He'd skipped along the asphalt like a rock and had road-burn all over his shoulder and back. It would be a while before his skin would heal and he was sure he'd have scars.

It didn't matter. The pain helped him focus on getting back. He'd acted as the rabbit to draw away the hounds. Now he needed to find out if his contact, Takashi Tanaka, had succeeded in making the drop, as promised.

The woman beside him cleared her throat. He glanced in her direction.

"Where are we going?" she asked.

"Gotta check on a friend."

"Could you drop me somewhere?"

The local authorities were already after him, thanks to the job his enemies had done impersonating federal law enforcement. It was a good long way to Lake George Village and every trooper between here and there was looking for him. If Takashi had gotten through, it would be simple, he could pick up the intel from the drop and return to base. If not, he needed to stay ahead of the law and the sleeper cell he knew would be after him just as soon as his captors failed to report in. Were they members of the organization Takashi had mentioned—Siming's Army, the Deathbringers?

"You still have your phone, Haley?" he asked. He already knew the answer. She didn't. "Maybe you can call the police for us?"

She hesitated at that, her mouth pursing. The woman was not only his savior, she was beautiful, and smart enough not to automatically believe him. Haley had light brown hair and intelligent blue eyes that were trying to work this out. Her brows arched as he debated if it was her full, tempting lips, the heart-shaped face or the widely spaced eyes that made her such a knockout. The sum of her parts, he decided, and the fact that she had literally picked him up off the road and taken out a spy with years of military training with a thermos. The man made a classic blunder, underestimating his opponent or perhaps not even recognizing that she was an opponent. Ryan knew that she was deciding her next move and she still had Needle's handgun.

If she pulled that gun on him, he'd have to kill her.

It was doubtful she still believed his detective bullshit and a second lie would be harder to believe. He'd put her in danger, but really, could she be in more trouble than she was now? If he left her, she was dead. And it would be a terrible, messy and painful death. If he took her, she might reduce his chances of reaching Lake George Village.

She deserved better but he had a mission to complete. Ryan had a bigger problem. The pain was no longer focusing him. It was blurring his vision.

Chapter Four

Ryan swiped at his eyes, but they failed to snap back into focus. In fact, the dark central tunnel in his field of vision was expanding,

"Where's that camp?"

"A...a ways. It's a hotel, lodge really."

A lie, he thought. The hesitation was a tell. He'd have to speak to her about that. Also she wouldn't meet his gaze, preferring to look at her now empty hands. The thermos lay in her lap, the bottom rim stained red. The handgun was likely in her pocket or purse. It seemed the thermos was her weapon of choice.

There were no hotels on this lake. He knew the terrain and his exact location. This Schroon Lake was connected to a larger one which bordered several small communities, but her GPS had said she was a few miles from her destination. The adventure camp was here, close by. But they couldn't stay there and he needed to ditch this car, fast.

What could he tell her that would keep them both alive?

He was mulling over if he should tell her another lie

or the truth. And if he told her the truth, how much did he need to reveal? She was going to live or die with him regardless of what he told her.

The important thing was that he do the best he could for her because she'd stopped for him. She'd saved him. And that made it hard to follow the directive to recover at all costs the flash drive containing the stolen intelligence on Siming's Army. His supervisors would tell him to leave her behind. She was a liability and her death meant nothing compared to the deaths of thousands.

But it meant something to him. He knew what Hornet and Needle would do to her. They'd never believe she wasn't involved. So they'd torture her and learn nothing. Collateral damage. The part of his heart that did not follow orders decided to bring her along. At least until he knew about Takashi. If Takashi had not succeeded in making the drop, Ryan needed to find him before their pursuers did.

"Hey!" she yelled.

He jerked his head up. Had he dozed off or passed out? Didn't matter. His vision was blurry and shaking his head did no good.

"Hold the wheel," he said.

The tension vibrated in her voice. "Why?"

"Because I'm going to pass out."

HALEY'S ABDUCTOR PROCEEDED to do just that, slumping backward and against the open window.

She lunged for the wheel but his foot remained on the

gas, the dead weight of his leg propelling them along too fast for this winding road.

Now what?

She didn't know but the upcoming turn in the road told her that she needed his foot off the gas or they were going off the road.

Again.

Haley imagined the federal agents following on foot and finding them wrapped around a tree. She used her opposite hand to shove for all she was worth, pushing until his foot slid from the gas pedal.

They glided easily around the turn, which required two hands on the wheel. Then they coasted to a stop on the dark road.

The heater blew and the engine rumbled. Through the vacant place where the rear window had been and broken windshield came the sound of the wind in the pine trees.

Why wasn't there anyone else on this blasted road?

She'd wanted to please her dad and so she'd done what he asked her, hoping she wouldn't disappoint him, wishing she could find the courage to step back into the stream of life, but knowing that was where the danger lay. Didn't this just prove her point?

Human wolves preyed on the weak and old, on drunk coeds. Police investigations revealed that her older sister spent as much time in bars as in the classroom. But her mother would not hear this. It went counter to her picture of her eldest daughter. In four days, Haley went from younger to only daughter. Of course she hadn't known that for five months. Five long, terrible months of worry over the missing.

She glanced over at the unconscious man beside her, illuminated only by the dashboard light. Blood oozed from the abrasions on his chest and shoulders, glistening in the blue glow from the dash. His head slumped down. She'd only seen this kind of musculature in action-adventure movies, when the hero somehow managed to lose his shirt or remove it for the female audience's sake. But this was real. He was real. She released her seat belt and placed a hand on his chest. His ribs rose and fell beneath her palm. His skin was too warm and damp with sweat.

Shock? The condition rose from her memory along with a list of symptoms and the emergency treatment for it.

Why she had ever thought premed was her life's passion was beyond her. She didn't even recognize that girl, the one who'd wanted the excitement of being a physician's assistant in a busy NYC emergency room. Being called to identify her sister's body had made it impossible to ever voluntarily visit a hospital again. Haley shuddered as sweat beaded cold on her forehead. No. Life-and-death situations were definitely not in her wheelhouse. At least not the death part.

Her heart beat painfully against her ribs and her throat burned.

"Oh, no you don't, Haley. You are not going to cry."

RYAN FELT THE pressure of someone's touch on his chest, the contact light and tentative. His eyes snapped open and he clamped his hand around the woman's wrist. She jumped and tugged in a vain effort to retrieve her captured appendage.

She could have shot him.

She could have left the car and made a run for it.

But she'd decided to check his condition instead. It wasn't wise. But it was kind. How long since he'd seen this sort of compassion?

"Haley," he whispered.

He released her. She rubbed her wrist with her opposite hand, not using either to hold the gun, which he knew she still had.

"What happened?"

"You fainted, I think."

"Passed out," he said and stretched backwards until his neck pressed to the headrest. "Marines don't faint."

"Is that what you are now? A Marine? Not a detective?"

He blew out a breath. "Once a Marine…"

She lifted her chin and gave him an appraising stare with those bright, intelligent eyes.

"Look, if I tell you the truth, chances are good you won't believe me. But if you are captured, you'll know that you died protecting your country."

"Um, I can't die. It will kill my mother."

"Then we have to get off the road."

She said nothing, but slipped her hand into her purse, leaving it there on what he suspected was the handle of the gun. He'd need to take that from her soon. But for now it seemed to make her feel safe. Chances were good that she'd make her escape attempt just as soon as she got out of the car.

"I have a cabin reserved close to here."

"They have your car."

"So?"

"So they'll find you there."

"That's impossible."

"By now they have your social media posts for the last decade. You didn't mention your plans there, did you?"

She said nothing. Of course she had.

"They know your home address because it is on the car rental agreement."

"How do you know it's a rental?"

"Bar code. Rear window."

"Who are they?"

"Mercenaries."

"Not mobsters or DEA. Now they are mercenaries?"

"Hired by a terrorist cell working within the US. Chinese, we think."

"They didn't look Chinese."

"Did they look like DEA agents?"

She dragged her white upper teeth over her lower lip and something inside him stirred with interest. He pushed it down.

"They shot at us. They didn't identify themselves. And they sure as hell didn't try to apprehend us."

She pressed her fist to her mouth and glanced out the ruined front window.

"They didn't do those things because they planned to

kill you and take me." He rubbed his tired eyes with a thumb and index finger. "Tell me where you are staying."

She explained about an adventure camp that her father had planned for her to try to get her to do something new and have a technology-free, screen-free adventure in nature.

"Mission accomplished. You've had an adventure. What did you think?"

"As expected. Hated it."

"How many cabins at the camp?"

"No idea."

"More than twelve?"

"Yes, I think so."

"All right. We'll start there. Resupply and then head out."

He counted the seconds during the long pause that followed. She was not planning to accompany him. Letting her slip away, thinking she'd escaped, would be best for one of them, but it wasn't her.

She spoke at last. "Out where?"

"I have to collect some intel left by my contact."

"I think I'd prefer to try the zip line."

He dropped his hand to his lap and faced her. "They're coming for us, Haley. And this time they will kill you."

Ryan drove to the entrance of the adventure camp.

"Registration is tomorrow but if you were arriving after eight, they said they'd leave the key inside on the kitchen counter."

They followed the signage to *Adirondacks Adven-*

tures and drove down a rutted dirt road, sighting the lake through the trees, glistening pale in the starlight.

"What number is your cabin?"

"They don't have numbers. I'm in Muskrat."

His brows lifted but he said nothing to this.

Two large poles flanked the road. Between them was a sign carved into a solid plank of varnished pine, each letter painted black. It read Welcome to Adirondacks Adventures!

They cruised past a series of metal frames encircling a grouping of four trampolines, a low rock-climbing wall and an open pavilion.

The lights were still on in the lodge, which sat at the top of the hill facing the glittering dark lake and the cabins that faced a large central grassy area. Ryan drove around the circular road that took him past four large log cabins with covered porches, identical except for the signage. They rolled past Moose, an accessible cabin complete with a wheelchair ramp in place of stairs. Then came Black Bear, Elk and Wolf. He continued on past the lake, dock and boat ramp. Beside the ramp, rows of overturned kayaks and canoes lay on the grass, awaiting the adventure campers.

On the opposite side sat the smaller single cabins. First was Muskrat.

"That's it," she said.

But Ryan continued to roll by, passing Possum, Rabbit, Otter, Beaver, Ermine, Red Squirrel and finally Raccoon, which was also an accessible cabin.

Ryan drove around a second time as Haley stared into the darkness beyond the porch of Cabin Muskrat.

It was doubtful they had found her location this quickly. But they'd be along.

"Detective Howard Insbrook?"

He didn't look at her as he spoke. "I'm no more a detective than you are. My name is Ryan Carr. I'm a government operative."

"Operative? You mean like in the Central Intelligence Agency?"

"That's the one."

"A spy?" she squeaked.

He shrugged. "I'm advising you not to run and not to scream when we leave this vehicle. Do you understand?" He turned his head and she nodded solemnly.

Ryan drew the stolen vehicle before the cabin designated Muskrat. When he left the auto his ribs were aching and the blanket he'd come away with was sticking to his skin. He got out and was on his way around to her, surprised that she hadn't already started her run or screamed for help. When he got to her side of the vehicle, he saw why.

Haley pointed a pistol at him.

Chapter Five

He had no time for Haley's shenanigans.

"Stop right there," she ordered. Her gun hand was unnervingly steady.

"You ever shot a gun?"

"Yes."

"Pistol?"

She shook her head.

"Back away," she ordered.

"You ever shoot a man, Haley?"

She pressed her lips together, looking determined. From somewhere across the way came the sound of conversation and then a woman's laughter. The other adventure campers were settling in.

"You have to flip the safety off or it won't shoot. It's right there." He extended his hand to point, never taking his eyes off her. But she took her eyes off him.

Haley's gaze dropped to the gun, turning it slightly in search of the safety.

Ryan did not even bother to strike her a blow. Instead, he captured her wrist and redirected the aim of the pistol skyward with one hand and removed it from her grip with the other.

He kept a hold on her as she made a vain effort to regain custody of the pistol, now well out of reach. Had she been a man, he would have punched her in the stomach or throat to make his point but, as Haley was female, tiny and his savior, he simply dragged her forward until she collided with his chest.

He meant the move as a way to get her attention and highlight that he was stronger, faster and more experienced. But when her soft body collided with his chest, stomach and hips, something unexpected happened.

The warning died on his lips as he took in the feel of her pressed up against him. She smelled wonderful, clean and floral. He inclined his head to inhale the sweetness of her hair and felt the stirring of attraction rippling through him.

Ryan's body's reaction caused him both dismay and irritation. He would never have sought out a little Good Samaritan with hair the color of a field mouse. Yet here he was, and his body definitely liked her well enough to become fully aroused. She must have felt it, his erection growing by the second, because she squeaked and tried to step back.

Little mouse, he thought again.

He wanted to press his opposite hand to her lower back and melt her closer to him, but the pistol in that hand and the clinking of wineglasses to his left drew him back to business.

Ryan dipped his head until his jaw was pressed to her forehead. His voice was a low growl as his lips moved close to the shell of her ear.

"We are leaving the vehicle and heading to the lodge.

If you try to run, I'll catch you. If you call for help, I'll have to kill whoever you involve. Do you understand?"

"Yes," she whispered, trembling.

He drew her under his arm, stooped to retrieve the blanket and wrapped it about them both. Her purse thumped against her hip as he guided her along the lakeshore, where he discovered that the canoes did not have paddles. He fixed his attention on the lodge, taking them past the dock and uphill behind the larger cabins. The area was neatly mown and each cabin had a large propane tank. There were lights from lanterns in both Wolf and Elk but the other residences appeared empty. A good place to sleep if not for the possible interruption by late arrivals and the fact that this was where Haley Nobel was expected to be. It was just a matter of time before his pursuers arrived to discover that car and set up perimeters accordingly.

As they reached the top of the hill, the lights flicked off in the lodge. This structure at least had electricity. A moment later a young man emerged wearing baggy pants gathered at the ankle, sandals and a T-shirt with the Sanskrit for *namaste* on his chest. He was white with an athletic build and his hair was styled in sun-bleached dreadlocks.

Ryan tugged Haley beside the Moose cabin. Just beyond, a group of people continued drinking and laughing. They were a poor choice for help, but if Haley planned to run or scream, now would be a great time.

He followed the direction of her gaze. She watched the young man as he swung along with a loose, care-free stride. With each step he moved farther from their position. Ryan tugged her close to his side and whispered, "Do you really want to be the cause of that young man's death?"

Haley made a sound in her throat that he interpreted as alarm but she did not cry out as they moved across the road and alongside the main lodge. He used the blanket to muffle the sound of his elbow breaking the windowpane that allowed him access to the lock. Once the window was open he lifted Haley through the gap and maintained control of her arm as he stepped inside behind her.

Either by design or accident, the young man had left a light on in the hallway that flanked the large fireplace on the right. So Ryan could see that they'd entered into the main meeting area, judging from the rows of folding chairs and a large central stone fireplace. To the left of the fireplace was a return station for trays and food, indicating a cafeteria beyond the closed double doors. To the right lay the lighted hallway. He assumed this led to restrooms and possibly an equipment storage facility.

He headed for the kitchen. He had not eaten since shortly before his capture earlier in the day and he was dehydrated and low on fuel. The kitchen door was flimsy and burst open with one kick. He dragged Haley along inside, closed the door behind them and then risked turning on the light.

"Food," he said and quickly located supplies. He filled his stomach with water straight from the tap of the large stainless steel sink. Next he located a tray of muffins, corn, blueberry and bran, along with a variety of breads.

He set the loaves of bread aside and ate two blue-berry muffins in rapid succession. When he looked up it was to find Haley staring at him in stunned silence.

"What?" he asked.

"When did you last eat?"

"Early this morning."

Her response was a sharp intake of breath. Then his little captive began scouring the walk-in refrigerator and brought him milk and orange juice. Kindness again. She was unexpected as sunshine in a cave.

"See if you can find portable food. Cereal, soup."

"Granola bars," she said, now standing before the stainless steel shelving. "Two kinds. Oh, and graham crackers. Hershey bars! And marshmallows. I remember these!"

He started putting supplies in a nylon bag he located hanging on a peg on the back wall beside some aprons. When the bag was full he moved on. He grabbed several dish towels and a carving knife, which he tucked into his rear pocket.

She had something in her hand, a white plastic case. "First-aid kit," she said.

"Take it and let's go."

He flicked off the light and they returned the way they had come. As predicted, the hallway yielded both a men's and women's bathroom.

"Um, I have to go," said Haley.

He motioned her toward the women's bathroom and surprised her by following her inside. Then he shut and locked the door and then flicked on the light.

"I can't go with you here."

"Your choice," said Ryan as he turned on both faucets in the sink. He used liquid soap to wash his face, hair and torso. Abrasions burned at the contact of the water. He did the best he could to scrub out the gravel and succeeded in making most of the abrasions bleed again.

Haley had decided to use the toilet after all and then joined him at the sink to wash her hands.

"Would you like me to wash the wounds on your back?"

In answer, he turned, presenting her with his back. Her touch was tentative at first. He flinched as she picked away pieces of gravel that tinged against the porcelain in the sink.

"Your back is covered with bruises," said Haley.

"Not the sort of treatment you'd expect from an agent from Federal Drug Enforcement," he replied.

He heard her pull of breath. Was she beginning to believe him?

"All they have is a hand dryer."

He rummaged in the supply bag and handed her a dish towel.

"You're bleeding," she said.

"I'd imagine so." He glanced at her in the mirror. Her brow was furrowed as she dabbed at his back.

"Ready?" he asked.

"For what?" She met his gaze in the mirror. "Are they really the bad guys?"

"I'm not letting you hang around to find out." He turned to face her, taking hold of her free hand. "I should leave you right here, Haley. It would increase

my chances of getting back to the drop. But I have absolutely zero doubt that, if I do that, you will be picked
up and tortured and killed."

Her eyes went wide at that. She shook her head.

"Seems a poor thank-you. The thing is, I can drag
you along with me. But I can't be on the lookout to keep
you from sneaking off. I'm going to need to sleep soon
and I can't take the risk of you giving away my position.
So you have a choice. Stay here and take your chances
or I'll bring you along and, if you don't slow me down,
I'll do my best to see you live through this."

She cocked her head and stared as if he'd sprouted
horns.

"How do I know if I can believe you?"

He shook his head. "What you witnessed back there
is my proof. Law enforcement officers don't behave
that way. You have to know that. So if they are not who
they say, maybe they are who I say. Mercenaries hired
by Siming's Army to recover the intelligence stolen by
my contact."

She was dragging her full lower lip through her teeth
again. It was distracting as all get-out.

He growled. "You can admit that they're dangerous."

"You're dangerous, too."

"True. Uncle Sam spent a lot of money to see that I
am...prepared for such situations. So, you coming or
staying?"

She glanced about as if the answer would materi-
alize in the small restroom. Confusion blanketed her
delicate features. Those eyes looked cobalt blue under
the artificial light.

Why had he given her the choice? He knew what his operations commander would tell him. She'd tell him to ditch this woman and never look back.

Haley drew a deep breath and he found himself holding his. Only at this second did he realize that he really wanted to keep her alive and with him. That made no sense. Was it because she had stopped to help him? Or because he wanted to kiss her?

That wasn't it, or wasn't all of it. He feared it was more.

"Okay, I'll come with you. But I have to call my dad."

He blew away his breath. "Let's go."

She handed the dish towel to him and pointed toward the blood running down his shoulder.

"I need to find a shirt." Ryan flicked off the light and they continued on to a locked room marked Equipment.

The padlock was solid but the connection to the frame and door was not. Ryan was inside in less than thirty seconds. With the door closed and the light on, he found what he was looking for. Climbing ropes, carabiners, chocks, helmets, backpacks, mess kits, flotation vests, archery equipment and paddles.

He paused at an acrylic box designed to sit on a counter and hold brochures. Inside, the bright yellow-and-green banner of the top pamphlet announced: Adventure Camp.

He lifted the brochure and read from the text. "Plenty of adventures await. Outdoors…"

He turned the bullet list to her. "You going to do all this?"

She glanced at the columns that had sent dread down her spine since Hanukkah.

Outdoors:
Hiking
Backpacking
Camping
Sleeping under the stars
Bouldering
Rock Climbing
Zip-lining
Aquatic:
Swimming
Boating
Canoeing
Kayaking
Jet Skis
White-water Rafting
Cliff Jumping

She planned to avoid every last one.

"Of course," she said, lifting her chin and daring him to refute her bravado.

He snorted and returned to loading a backpack with the food bag, a small camping stove, two fuel tanks and a mess kit. To this, he added two small nylon tents.

"Did you have to provide sleeping bags?" he asked.

"Yes."

He took two bed pads and tied them on the top of the pack. "Get another pack," he said.

She selected one and brought it to him. He added

rope, headlamps and arrows. To his pack he tied an archery bow. The weapon was meant for recreation but in the right hands it was silent and it could be deadly. He shook out a woolen army blanket and sliced a slit in the center, transforming it into a poncho, which he slipped over his head.

"See if you can find matches or a lighter." He located hiking maps and a guidebook to the Adirondack hiking trails and added these to his bundle. He tried to find two-way radios but settled for bug spray, sunscreen, a compass and a small folding shovel.

"What are these?" Haley said, lifting bug coils.

"Take those," he said.

By the time he had the packs ready she had not found matches so they left without them. He used the main entrance to leave the lodge and returned the way they had come. He left both packs and Haley outside the first cabin as he used his blanket to break the back window. Once inside, he found himself in a bedroom that contained two sets of bunk beds. Upon each bunk was a rolled mattress too heavy to bring along and on the box springs sat a pillow, too big to bring along. There were also clean sheets in plastic containers and, bingo, a woolen blanket. He took two blankets and continued on to the kitchen. In the cabinet drawer he found a box of matches. He also purloined a can opener and small paring knife, two spoons, two forks and, from the tinderbox beside the fireplace, a small dull hatchet.

He half expected to find Haley gone when he returned, but she was there, her long neck stretched to full extension and her head swiveling back and forth.

Ryan added his new collection of gear to the second pack and helped Haley shoulder the load. He led her down behind the cabins to the lakeshore.

At the lakefront the water gently lapped the mud and gravel beyond the waiting canoes and kayaks, neatly stored on racks. If he were traveling alone he would have selected a kayak. It was sleeker, faster and required less effort to paddle. However, with Haley along, he instead selected a canoe, rolling it upright and sliding it half into the water. From there he took the pack Haley carried and placed it to the center of the canoe. He added his own pack beside hers so as to balance the load. Then he motioned to Haley.

"Time to go," he said.

But Haley was backing away.

Ryan released the canoe and took two steps toward her. "Haley?"

She was shaking her head. "I can't go with you. I can't… I don't know what's happening but I'll wait until you leave. Totally out of sight before I call the police."

He lifted a hand toward her in a signal to stop and to come and to not make him responsible for this decision. He knew he was not going to force her into the canoe but he knew equally well that if he left her here on the lakeshore, she was sure to die.

"Haley, you can't call the police. They'll turn you over to those men. They're good. Professionals. You won't be able to tell the difference between them and the real thing. Neither will the locals. You have to trust me. I know it stinks, but I'm your only chance."

"Ryan, no offense. But I don't know you. I don't

know what you're involved in but I can't be involved in it. My dad already paid for this camp. He wants me to get out there and try new things. He thinks... He thinks... I just have to go."

"All right, Haley. I'm sorry for involving you in this. And I'm sorry you won't come with me."

She was backing away. Her cautious expression told him that she did not quite believe that he would let her simply leave.

"Take care," she said.

He pushed the canoe farther into the water so that the front end became buoyant and only the back tip of the canoe was in contact with the shore. Then he added both paddles and pushed off. He held the gunwales and seated himself low on the bottom of the canoe. Making himself a smaller target. He used his fingernails to pop off three of the stick-on numbers that identifed the canoe and then lifted a paddle. He was already ten feet from the shore. Haley was a dark silhouette standing silent and motionless on the shoreline. He looked beyond her up the row of smaller cabins and noticed the glint of starlight on a metal roof. There was a vehicle parked in the gravel lot shared by Muskrat, Possum and Rabbit cabins. The vehicle had not been on-site when they entered the lodge.

Haley was moving now, back toward the cabin she had been assigned.

He could not call back to her and should not return for her. She'd made her choice. A bad choice, but hers, nonetheless. So he was going to paddle away and let the woman who saved his life walk into the jaws of death.

Seemingly of its own volition the paddle cut a clean edge through the lake water, turning the canoe back toward shore.

Chapter Six

Haley watched the canoe cut through the water, his strokes smooth and graceful. You would never know by looking at the dark form in the silent canoe that the man was bruised, battered and bleeding. She almost wished she had gone with him.

"Don't be ridiculous, Haley. He's better without you and you are way better without him. Your mistake was stopping in the first place." She didn't know what had gotten into her. She had a very strict policy about almost everything, including the folly of Good Samaritans.

Haley was aware that the serial killer, Ted Bundy, had used a fake arm cast to lure young women into helping him move furniture into his van. Once inside the van, they were never seen by friends or family again.

She thought about Maggie, as she always did when faced with possible violence or danger. Had Maggie been picked up by someone who'd offered help or had she been snatched from the street?

She wondered again about her sister's last moments. Thinking about her sister's time in captivity was the worst part.

"No, the worst part is never seeing her again."

Haley turned toward the smaller cabins, walking past the dock and the terrifyingly small kayaks reaching the gravel road that would take her to Cabin Muskrat. She paused when she noticed the black van parked between Muskrat and Rabbit. A quicksilver flash of alarm lifted every hair on her body. Her skin tingled with apprehension. That van had not been there when she and Ryan had toured past the cabins.

She didn't like vans in general and especially did not like vans that had no rear windows and only a single sliding side door. It was not the sort of vehicle that adventure campers might use. Now her heart sledgehammered in her chest as she glanced back to the lake. There was no sign of Ryan. She took a step backward, trying to decide if she should run toward the lake, toward the badly damaged vehicle they had left before the Moose cabin or return to the lodge.

The passenger door of the van opened and the overhead light flicked on. She caught a glimpse of a big muscular man dressed in dark clothing before the door clicked shut and the light blinked off. Was that the man Ryan had choked out? How did he get here so darn fast?

She took another step backward and heard a footfall on the porch of Cabin Muskrat. Was that a figure standing at the rail?

"No. No. No," she whispered as both hands pressed to her mouth. She glanced back to the car across the central green and uphill. The lake was downhill but she had no paddle and doubted she could get away by diving into the water. She could swim, but was a poor swimmer at best.

The man beside the van crept forward, gravel crunching beneath his heels.

"Haley Nobel?" The question came from the dark space of the porch. There was no doubt now. Someone was waiting for her at her cabin. Haley took one step backward, preparing to run, when she heard an unfamiliar sound.

Phfft.

The man on the porch gave a groan and then toppled forward over the porch rail, landing on the grass beside the steps with a thud.

Haley's eyes bulged as she spotted the arrow protruding from the man's back.

Ryan. It had to be.

She glanced about but saw no one.

The second man was running toward her now, arms extended. She stumbled backward two steps before falling to her rear end. Only then did she realize that her pursuer aimed a pistol at her. But as he rounded the edge of the cabin Ryan appeared from the darkness, vaulting from the steps and onto the man's back. She saw the silver flash of a knife blade. Her pursuer dropped to his knees, both hands clutching his throat. The gurgling sound told Haley that something terrible had happened. She scrambled to her feet. Ryan was already moving toward the man who had toppled from the porch. Ryan dropped to one knee and with a quick, efficient movement of his arm slit the man's throat.

Haley gained her feet, turned tail and ran. She did not

run with a destination in mind. She did not run with a plan but she did run for her life. She was somewhere between the canoes and the Wolf cabin when Ryan caught her and brought her to the ground. His hand went to her mouth and his lips went to her ear.

"Quiet now, there may be more of them."

She nodded so he would know she understood. Slowly his fingers dragged from her mouth. She was choking on sobs as he gathered her close, holding her to his chest, cradling her as he rocked her, whispering to her as she clung and sobbed.

"It's okay, Haley. I got you. I won't leave you again."

She couldn't speak, could barely breathe. Ryan stroked her hair, rubbed her back and made quiet sounds of comfort. At last she tipped her head back, looking into dark unfathomable eyes.

She trembled, clinging like a lost child. "It was them. You told me. You warned me. I didn't believe. I didn't believe that they'd come for me. How did you know that they'd find me?"

She was babbling, rambling, chattering like a monkey, but she could not seem to stop. He drew her gently to her feet.

"Not the same men, but the same organization."

"How did they find me so fast?"

But she knew. If anyone in the world knew how simple it was to locate, track and intercept a person who was hooked into social media, it should be her. It was how she made her living, finding and exploiting weaknesses.

Ryan wrapped a strong arm around her shoulders and guided her down to the lakeshore, past the canoes on the dock, the kayaks and into the tall reeds where his canoe waited. This time she gave him no argument as he scooped her into his arms and carried her through the knee-deep water, depositing her onto the small seat at the front of the canoe.

He offered her a paddle. "Ever use one of these?"

She shook her head, accepting the smooth wooden paddle and holding it upright before her, choking the neck in sweaty hands.

"Just hold on to it for now. Grab the gunnels," he whispered.

"The whats?"

"Sides of the canoe. I'm shoving off."

Haley gave a little cry as the canoe moved beneath her. She dropped the paddle and it banged against the metal frame, the sound loud as a gong in the still night. Haley stretched her arms out to grasp the gunnels as mud and gravel scraped the bottom beneath her. Ryan stepped inside and gave one last push with his foot to send them into deeper water.

Ryan gained his seat as Haley looked back toward the camp. She saw someone wading out to his hips.

"Ryan!" she yelled, pointing.

He turned. Simultaneously, she saw the muzzle flash and heard the pop of a gunshot. Ryan spun on the metal seat, bringing both hands together, and returned fire. The man dropped into the water. At first she thought he was moving behind the dock for cover, but the complete silence had her skin crawling. Ryan waited, pistol aimed and ready, but no target presented itself as they drifted farther along the shore.

Then she saw it, the large object floating motionless in the water, and she knew that shooter would not be coming after them. Ryan held his position, motionless, patient.

Finally, he lifted his paddle and scooped it through the dark water beside the canoe, sending them forward and out of sight of the camp and Cabin Muskrat where two corpses lay in the front lawn and one floated in the lake.

Looked like her adventures were well underway.

THEY HAD NOT been seen but it would not take a mastermind to recognize that three men had arrived in a van but the drivers of the bullet-riddled sedan were missing along with gear and a single canoe. They would be looking for at least one person, likely two. He assumed they would do a sweep of the cabins beginning in close proximity and working outward. Roadblocks would be erected. Vehicles would be searched and identification checked. His most pressing problem was that he was nodding off as he paddled. He had spent the better part of the day tied to a folding chair getting pummeled between rounds of questioning. It had taken time to convince them that he had hidden the flash drive when in fact, he had never collected it from Takashi, choosing instead to lead them in the opposite direction to give the other operative time to make the drop as planned. Then he could return to Lake George to collect the goods. Unfortunately he was the only one besides Takashi who knew where to look and that was only if Takashi had survived long enough to make the drop. His failure to report in would signal trouble but that would not tell them where to look for him, Takashi or the flash drive.

Ryan pulled for all he was worth. How long until the local sheriff arrived and took his boat out to look for night paddlers?

He figured he had maybe two hours.

"You came back for me," she said, her words drifting to him on the cold, crisp air.

He glanced toward her position. She sat hunched on the seat, hugging the paddle as her entire body vibrated with tremors. He wished he could take her in his arms again. It had felt right, too darn right, he realized. This little woman was rapidly becoming more distracting.

"Will they come after us?"

"The police?"

"No, the other ones. The ones chasing us."

"I don't know how to break it to you but three more of their guys are KIA. Everyone, from the state police to their guys, will be after us."

"KIA?" she asked.

"Killed in action. Dead."

She nodded and then tried to paddle but she had her paddle on the same side as him. If the stroke had been a good one it would have turned them. Instead, it nearly rocked her into the lake.

She gasped and pulled back her paddle as if afraid to try again.

"Other side. Paddle opposite me. I'm switching every third stroke. Match your strokes to mine and don't lean."

"No leaning. Got it."

And she did. Within three cycles she had the timing

down and was doing an effective job conveying them. She had a natural coordination and grace. Even in the starlight, she was a pleasure to watch in motion.

"Done this before?" he asked.

"As a kid. My dad used to take me and my sister…" Her words dropped off. He waited but she said nothing more.

He took them well south of the camp and then out across the lake. Here they would be most vulnerable cutting across the reflective surface of the lake. But he knew the law enforcement officers and first responders would begin their search at the camp and that roadblocks would be erected on Route 9 as soon as the dead were mistakenly identified as DEA agents. It would take a day or so for them to realize these men were not what they seemed but by then the hounds would be back on their trail with everything they had. He knew they had both drones and helicopters at their disposal.

Ryan headed for the small community of Adirondack on the east side of Schroon Lake. From there he needed to make it the fifteen miles to Lake George. Unfortunately those fifteen miles were rough and rugged wilderness area that would skirt around Pharaoh Lake and up and over Pharaoh Mountain.

First priority was to hide this canoe and leave it behind. They glided silently along. Only the pull of the paddle made a sucking sound and created tiny whirlpools in its wake. Water lapped gently against the sides of the metal canoe. This lake was over two miles in length, a narrow finger with two wider knuckles. The inlet was to his north; the outlet was to his south. If he

were the one predicting course he would have aimed
for the outlets at the south end and set up a perimeter
accordingly.

Ryan dipped his hand into the icy lake water and
splashed it onto his face, hoping the cold and wet would
help rouse him. His brain felt fuzzy as if his head were
filled with cotton. They'd hit him in the head more than
once, so he assumed this was the result of a concussion
and hoped he wasn't bleeding into his cranium.

The dark outline of the lakeshore drew nearer with
every stroke of his paddle. Haley said nothing but continued industriously pulling with the paddle. She was
naturally athletic and coordinated, recalling the physical motion quickly.

He drew them alongside a protruding dock. Set in
the pines he could see the glint of moonlight off glass.
A lake house, he suspected. The canoe slid to a halt as
he caught the edge of the dock.

"Can you step out?" he asked.

"I think so," she replied. Haley gathered herself on
the seat, gripping her paddle, and smoothly stepped
onto the dock. He dragged the canoe slightly forward
and asked her to retrieve the packs. Once they were
both unloaded, he continued on to the shore, paddling
quickly to help drive the front end of the canoe up
onto the gravel bank. There he exited the canoe and
brought it the rest of the way ashore. Haley waited on
the dock for him. He helped her carry the gear to the
canoe and instructed her to wait for him. She ducked
down low, following his instructions exactly. He had

no concerns that she would run off. Not after what she had witnessed—three men coming for her.

Ryan made a quick perimeter sweep. The lake house was ample. Beside the house was a canoe. He decided to add their canoe to this one. Hoping the removed numbers and the existing canoe would allow his conveyance to hide in plain sight.

He returned for Haley, upending the canoe and carrying it over his head. Haley carried one pack and followed him. She helped him place the canoe silently beside the house.

"Are we staying here?" she asked.

"No, they're going to search empty buildings for us. They'll start on the west side but they'll get around to this place and I need rest. We need to make camp in a place they will not find us."

"Where's that?" she asked.

"Haley, I need to get back to the place where my contact left the package. He gave me the location this morning in person before we were separated. I have to head for that spot."

Ryan collected the second pack and then took them up the driveway, then followed the road that hugged the lakeshore's east bank, heading north. He used his headlight to consult the map and then flicked it off again. They hiked in silence under the cover of the pines. The road was paved and narrow, created solely to provide access to the residences on this side of the mountain lake. The golf course marked the narrowest part of the lake and a stream that would take them eventually to the Pharaoh Lake trail. This way was rough with no maintained road or hiking trail. Going was slow, but he knew the forest would make them disappear. He continued on until Haley's lungs heaved like a bellows and she began to stagger and weave.

"Okay. We'll camp here."

Haley folded at the waist placing her palms on her knees as she gasped. She straightened as he helped her remove her pack. He brought them to the base of a large white pine, knowing its wide branches and thick needles would keep any rain or dew off them. As Haley's breathing slowed her teeth began to chatter. Without the exertion of the hiking her damp clothes were cooling her skin and making her shiver.

"Cross hiking off the adventure camp list," she said.

He chuckled but Haley's expression was grim.

Ryan removed his pack and quickly set to work erecting one of the tents, his vision going in and out of focus. It was designed to be a single-person tent only large enough for one man and one sleeping bag. He handed Haley a water bottle as he turned back to the tent, placing both pads down and then rolling out both blankets. He sat beside her, sharing the granola bars she had discovered. He sipped the water sparingly. When he snapped awake, he realized that he could postpone sleep no longer. He used the last of his waning energy to throw one end of the climbing rope over a branch of an oak tree some fifty feet from their camp and hauled up their packs into the leafy canopy.

"Why are you doing that?" she asked.

"Keep the bears and 'coons out of our food supplies."

Her body went rigid and her shivering momentarily

ceased. "Bears? Did you say bears?" She pointed at his tent. "I'm not sleeping on the ground with bears."

"Where would you like to sleep?"

"My apartment but barring that..." She pointed straight up.

"I have the guns from three of our attackers and you have the fourth. We don't have to worry about bears."

"Well, that's one thing off the list. Should I set up the other tent?"

"If you like, or we can sleep together in this one."

She shifted her gaze from the tent to him and then back to the tent. He tried to remain professional as his body responded naturally to the prospect of having Haley's small, curvy body pressed to his. He thought he did a commendable job of keeping his expression serene as his heart rate and breathing accelerated.

Haley eyed him cautiously and then looked at the tent.

"Kind of small. Isn't it?"

"Keep the bugs off us and I can keep you warm."

"I'd imagine so." She had her hands on her hips. "I'll sleep out here."

"No, you won't. The bugs will eat you alive."

"There aren't any bugs," she said, arms lifted.

"It's too cold now. But in the early morning, they'll come. Biting flies and mosquitoes."

Still she hesitated.

"Haley, you're cold. I'm exhausted. I need to sleep so you decide. I'm going inside."

He crawled into the narrow tent and rolled his blanket poncho as a pillow. Then he slipped under the other blankets. He left the tent unzipped. He could hear her stamping her feet and the sound of the castanets that her teeth had become. He had not intended to drop to sleep but he did, leaving her outside the tent with her indecisions.

Chapter Seven

Haley stood outside the tiny tent with her arms wrapped tight about herself and her teeth tapping together as if sending some distress signal via Morse code. She was positive that she would not be able to erect her tent alone in the dark, with or without a headlight. She was also fairly certain that she would be unable to loosen and lower the two packs he had tied so neatly up and out of sight.

"Ryan?" She waited but received no answer. She inched closer to the tent, listening. From within the flimsy nylon she heard a soft snoring. The man was already asleep. And he had both blankets!

Above her in the pine tree came the scratching of tiny claws. She flipped on her headlight and searched the tree canopy but saw nothing. Her heart was now slamming into her ribs. She lifted the beam higher and then she saw it. About twelve inches in length with eyes as big and black as twin marbles. The coat was gray on top and, judging from the thin, pink, hairless tail, it looked to belong to the rodent family. Haley blew out a breath.

"To heck with this." Haley scrambled into the tent,

pausing only to zip the closures. There was no room to sit up. She hunched at the lower end of the tent. The frame held the nylon approximately three feet at its highest in the center above Ryan's head. She crawled along beside him, stretching out on the padding. It was then she realized that he was using his makeshift poncho as a headrest and had both blankets up to his chin. But she knew his chest was bare under that and the knowledge accompanied the image of his muscular form.

She exhaled against the kick of desire.

"Oh, gosh." Haley was not inexperienced with men, but all her encounters involved safe, carefully vetted men who were as harmless as bunny rabbits. Now it seemed she shared a tent with a tiger.

She pressed her lips together and exhaled a long dragon's breath as she debated the wisdom of yanking the third blanket out from under his head as her shivering grew worse. She shone her light on Ryan's face. His cheek was bruised and swollen. The gash at his hairline looked painful, the dark scab already forming. His eyes squeezed shut and then one flicked open. He lifted a hand to shade his eyes from her light. Then he lifted one side of the blankets to her. Her headlight's beam illuminated the pale length of exposed male flesh. The angry purple bruises glowed on his ribs. How had he paddled and hiked and shot an arrow at the guy that came to kill her?

"Come here, Haley, so we can rest." His voice was low and sexy.

She swallowed her reservations, or tried to, only to discover her throat was too dry.

Haley was certain of his intentions. He wanted to sleep and to keep her warm and safe. It wasn't his fault that just a glimpse of him made all systems go haywire.

She flicked off her light and unlaced her boots. Then she slipped beneath the blankets beside him, lying on her side with one leg resting on his muscular thigh and one hand hugging the thick bicep. He smelled of sweat and blood and pine.

She closed her eyes and wondered if she had ever been this tired in her life. Ryan's snore reassured. They were safe for the moment.

"Camping," she whispered, mentally checking off one more item of the adventure camper's list.

Haley smiled and then dropped off to sleep almost immediately, without her iPod playing the Italian opera she used to tempt sleep, without her app to create the soothing sounds of the ocean or rain or a faraway train whistle. She also stayed asleep, missing her customary late-night panic attacks where she woke covered in sweat and trembling. At such times she would rouse from bed, use the bathroom, make a cup of tea and settle in to read in bed until her eyes dropped closed at last. Haley had tried anything and everything to keep herself from dwelling on her sister's horrific death. Nothing worked except, apparently, exhaustion mixed with Ryan Carr.

SHE WOKE TO find the daylight filtering through the fabric of the nylon tent, casting them both in blue. She now lay on her side with him spooning her. His knees bent so his thighs pressed to the back of her legs. One of his arms wrapped around her waist, his forearm pressed to her sternum and his hand splayed over her upper chest. She found his embrace one of support, rather than sensuality. But other parts of him made her skin tingle. His breathing told her he was sleeping, each soft exhalation fanning the crown of her head. But his body was aroused, his erection pressing to the soft flesh of her backside. Her eyes widened but she lay still. She didn't know what surprised her more, her own response to his sleeping seduction or the recognition that she had not spent half the night trying and failing to fall asleep. She had experienced no nightmares and felt rested despite the soreness across her shoulders, which she attributed to the paddling and carrying the heavy pack.

Something about his heart beating slow and steady and his breath brushing her skin made her relax. He shifted his hips, increasing the pressure between them and she rolled to her back.

His eyes snapped open and shifted. He lifted his head to listen and then lowered it back to the thick pillow of his folded arm. He moved the opposite hand and his fingers formed the sign of *okay*.

She nodded.

"What woke you?" he asked.

Her face heated and she was certain the blush reached from her forehead to her toes.

He smiled and rolled to his back.

"Bladder?"

"Yeah," she admitted. Her shoulder and arm slipped

from the cover of the blankets and she was surprised at the chill in the air.

"Brrr," she said, sinking deeper into the blankets they shared. The fit was tight, and she had to roll toward him to remain inside the cocoon of warmth. She lifted to an elbow to look down at him.

The redness beneath his eyes had gone and his sleepy smile made promises she half hoped he'd keep. His scruffy cheeks were now looking more like a beard than a five o'clock shadow. His crisp haircut had failed on the top, making his hair tousled. She smoothed it back in place with a sweep of one hand. His smile widened.

"What time do you think it is?" she asked.

He glanced at the tent canopy. "Maybe eight in the morning. Six-to-seven straight hours of shut-eye. I needed that. But we have to get going."

He stretched, his feet and hands touching opposite ends of the tent. He wasn't very tall, average, but much bigger than her. She'd say he was about five feet, ten inches in height.

"I think it's time for you to tell me what is happening," she said.

"Soon as I get back." He threw off the blanket and pushed himself to a seated position. Now he sat hunched in the small quarters, giving her an eye-popping view of his muscular chest and impossibly ripped abdomen. The man was a walking advertisement for protein powder.

"Be right back," he said. He grabbed the poncho blanket and his boots before unzipping the tent flap and slipping away. She saw his shadow move along the nylon tent fabric before he disappeared with the rustle into the woods.

Haley took the opportunity to locate her boots and replace them before following him from the tent. She was shivering as she replaced her thin jacket and stepped out to face the day. First order of business was to relieve herself. When she returned to the camp area it was to find Ryan squatting before a stove hardly bigger than a water thermos. Atop the single burner sat a small aluminum pan half filled with water.

"I have water filters, so we do not have to conserve water. I'm heating this so we can wash up. Then I'll heat some more water for oatmeal."

"You found oatmeal?" The man knew the way to a woman's heart.

He again wore the blanket poncho. Now all she had to contend with was his handsome face, charming smile and the sympathy raised from the cuts and bruises on his forehead and cheek. He dipped a bandanna into the aluminum pots and handed the warm wet cloth to her. She washed her face and handed it back.

"I can give you some privacy if you'd like to wash anything else."

Her face flushed again and she dropped the contact of their gaze. Still unable to meet his eyes, she nodded.

He rose to his feet, gathered his pack and set off out from the cover of the white pine.

"Don't be long," he said.

She waited only until he was out of sight and then used the cloth to wash her torso under her shirt, giving quick attention to the rest of her. He returned to wash his face. When he dragged the poncho over his head and stood with the cloth to wash his arms, she stood to give him privacy as well. Then she noticed again the abrasions across his shoulders and back.

"Would you like me to give those a wash?"

He handed her the cloth and folded to his seat, sitting cross-legged before the little single-burner stove. She gently lifted the cloth, wrung out the excess water and began the slow process of washing away the dirt and grime that covered his naked upper body. As she worked she allowed herself to become familiar with his taut skin and the tiny mole below his left shoulder blade. There was a thread-thin white scar across his lower back. She traced it with her finger and his skin puckered.

"You're killing me, you know?" He wiped his palm over his mouth. "Hard enough to sleep beside you all night, but this is a new form of torture."

She smiled, resting a hand on one broad shoulder. "The oldest sort, I believe."

He chuckled.

She drew one finger along the scar again. "How did you get this?"

"Knife wound after engaging the enemy."

"Where?"

"I can't tell you."

She finished washing his back and moved before him, handing him the cloth. His hand captured hers and drew it to his chest, pinning her there.

"What can you tell me?" she asked.

"I can tell you what they already know."

Haley felt a chill nestle at the base of her spine. Telling her only what his opponents already knew was a way to ensure that she could not reveal any of his secrets. She drew her hand free and deposited the cloth back in the aluminum pan. He retrieved it and then began methodically washing beneath his arms and across his chest as he spoke.

"My assignment was to collect intelligence from a foreign agent, a courier, who delivered it across the Canadian border. This intel came directly from the men who hired the mercenaries pursuing us now. They know the contents of the intel and will do anything to prevent it from reaching US government officials."

Haley shifted, suddenly uneasy.

The normal sounds of insects and the branches of the trees creaking together as they moved in the morning breeze suddenly seemed more ominous. The sunshine filtering down in great beams all about them served to reveal their position. She almost missed the night.

"What does the intel look like?" She asked.

"I believe it is a simple flash drive. Do you know what that is?"

She smiled. "Ryan, I make my living with computers. Private contractor."

"What do you do, tech help?"

"The opposite. I'm paid by corporations, utilities and the US government to locate and exploit weaknesses in their network security systems."

"You're a hacker?"

She worked for various entities as an independent contractor with a very specific skill set. But she wasn't telling Ryan that she was paid by DHS and the Defense Department to expose and exploit vulnerabilities in their firewalls and then to seal them up.

"Consultant." She smiled at the look of respect and surprise now spreading across his features.

"Well, I'll be."

"So I not only know what a thumb drive is, I know how to access files from a corrupted Master Boot Record, PBR or directory structure. And I can figure out if the corruption is physical or logical due to malware, bad sector or file system or inaccessible drives, for example."

"Any other hidden talents?"

"I'm in the top 100 for *World of Warcraft* and I'm fifth in *Counter-Strike*, look out Doltnugget06."

"There's more than one Doltnugget?"

"Apparently."

"What's your gamer name?"

She looked away. "You don't have the security clearance for that one."

His smile said he accepted the challenge as he smoothly changed the subject.

"You seem very fit for someone who spends so much time online."

"I went to college on a tennis scholarship and worked part-time in my dad's landscaping biz. He's a landscape architect."

As a teenager, she worked every summer on so many job sites customers thought she was a regular part of his crew. She may as well have been. She could operate any of the heavy machinery he owned.

"Planting flowers?" he asked.

"Operating the backhoe, mostly, and the Bobcat."

His brows rose in speculation at this revelation.

"I also am a regular at my neighborhood gym. It's dope."

"Goat yoga?" he asked, but the uncertainty in his tone told her that he no longer was so certain that he could read her at a glance.

She laughed. "Tae kwon do. Green belt."

His brows lifted high on his broad forehead. "You are full of surprises."

"Same goes for you, 007."

"I hope my courier got away. If not there won't be a package to recover and deliver to headquarters."

Haley folded into a seat, crossing her legs freestyle before her and resting her hands in her lap.

"If it's so important, why send one man to recover it?"

"It's how it's done. The less attention drawn to our business, the better."

"If you are a central intelligence agent, you are not supposed to be conducting operations on US soil. Isn't that correct?"

"We operate worldwide."

She made a face.

"How are you going to reestablish communications with your courier?"

"I don't need to. He gave me the drop location."

"Where?" She asked.

Ryan shook his head.

He wouldn't tell her because that was a detail that his pursuers did not know.

"Once we reach the hiking trail, wouldn't it be safer for me to just go in the opposite direction?" she asked.

"Not if they happen to be in the opposite direction. They know what you look like, Haley. They're coming after you, the same as they're coming after me. I'm your only chance. I'm not saying it's a great chance but it is all you've got."

Ryan dumped the water from the pot, selected a smaller frying pan, added water and increased the flame height.

"Apple and cinnamon or maple walnut?" He asked, holding up two small packets of oatmeal.

"Apple."

He returned the maple walnut packet to the bag and collected three similarly colored pouches. When the water began a slow boil he reduced the flame and tore open the packets, adding them one at a time as he stirred with a wicked-looking knife.

"I think we have a spoon somewhere," she said.

"Save it for eating." He drew out a plastic cup. "Now, how about you explain why your dad thinks that you need summer camp at the age of..."

Haley pursed her lips but then answered. "The age of twenty-three."

The oatmeal thickened. Ryan slopped a third of the breakfast into a cup and handed it over with a plastic spoon. He ate his from the pan with a second spoon.

He lifted his brows and blew on his meal, waiting.

Haley wondered how much to tell him.

"I've been having a rough time."

"Why?"

"I just don't feel safe. I spend a lot of time inside with my work and I don't go places I don't know. I don't make new friends or really have much of a social life."

"That's concerning, especially to a father. Any reason?"

She held her untouched oatmeal in her cupped hands as she looked away, up to the bright green leaves that blocked the sunlight and the lacework of branches overhead.

"Haley?"

Chapter Eight

Haley unlocked her jaw, ignored the pain twisting her stomach and spoke. "My sister, Maggie, was murdered five years ago."

His hand was on her shoulder now, giving a squeeze. She told herself not to cry but the great racking sobs bubbled up as tears rolled down her cheeks, as if on a conveyer belt.

He set aside his breakfast and gathered her into his lap. She curled against him, clutching the coarse blanket he wore and burying her cheek in the musty wool weave.

"I'm so sorry, Haley." He stroked her head, lowering his mouth so that his words were a whispered caress against her temple. "What happened?"

The great jumble of emotions flashed through her with thoughts of the police reports, missing persons photos, news reporters. It was all a tangle and she did not like to go back there, but she carried it with her every day.

"She'd just graduated from Skidmore College. She had her first job in Brooklyn on a PR team for a consortium of local businesses in an area called DUMBO. Do you know it?"

"Down Under the Manhattan Bridge Overpass. I've worked there."

"Right!" she brightened until she recalled what she still had to put into words. "Maggie had her first place in Williamsburg. Nice building. Nice neighborhood. She and her new coworkers went out on a Friday night on Bedford Avenue and got separated. Maggie didn't come home. My family went a little crazy. We were on the news, in the papers. Hired a private investigator. Hounded the police. That was November. Christmas that year was…" She shook her head. "No word, no leads. She just vanished. We were called for a Jane Doe in early January. Not her."

He rubbed her back and she struggled to control her breathing, blowing out a long breath.

"Her body was located in late January, less than a mile from where she disappeared." Haley covered her face for this part. "Near the water in a shallow grave on the East River between a park and an old warehouse. I made the identification, her clothes and bag, calf-high boots that she loved."

"You IDed her?"

She pressed her hand over her mouth as the bite of oatmeal she'd sent down threatened to come back up. The cold air helped keep it down.

"Yes. She'd been stabbed multiple times, murdered. The cold preserved her so we learned she'd been bound and some of the bruises were several days old. I don't know how they know that but someone kept her. We don't know for how long."

"Oh, Haley." He wrapped her in his strong arms.

He'd been a Marine, he said. Had he lost friends while serving his country?

"Since then, I just can't seem to find myself. It's like part of me died that night, too. And I can't risk anything happening to me. I saw what that did to my parents. If I got killed, it would kill them."

"Why do you say you died?"

"I'm different, scared of things I never was before. Second-guessing decisions, staying where I'm safe."

"Brooklyn? Some would argue that's not very safe."

"I'm in a good neighborhood, a building with a good security system, it's…" *Mine*, she almost said, but stopped herself.

"Where are your parents?"

"Dad is still in Colonie, that's near Albany. But Mom moved down to Beacon, NY, after they divorced."

"Divorced because of your sister's death?"

She nodded. "How did you know?"

"It happens."

Haley slipped back off his lap, feeling awkward all of a sudden. She lifted her cup, stirring the lumpy cold glue that had recently been a tempting meal.

He ate all of his meal with efficiency as she toyed with hers. Swallowing was hard but she tried.

"Why Brooklyn?"

"My work is there."

"Your work is anywhere and everywhere."

"True."

"So why Brooklyn?"

She tucked her chin and whispered her answer. "It's Maggie's old place. She had been there two months and…"

"You moved into her apartment?"

Haley nodded.

"I was supposed to clean it out but I just…stayed."

She nodded, squeezing her eyes shut.

"I see why your dad is worried."

"That's not why. I just, I agreed to clean out her place, so they wouldn't have to and I… I just couldn't."

"What was she like?" he asked.

Before she knew it Haley was bubbling with stories about the mischief they had gotten into and the family adventures. Skiing in the Adirondacks in the winter, sailing on Otsego Lake in the summer. The two rode horses, competing in jumping and cross-country courses. Maggie did gymnastics and Haley played tennis on their high school teams.

"One year we went to Lake Placid and got to try the luge. It was summer but they let you run part of the course on sleds with wheels. I crashed, but Maggie made it all the way down."

"Crashed?"

She nodded, lifting her head to grin, and thrust up her jacket sleeve to show him a small scar on her elbow.

"Sounds like you two were a couple of daredevils."

But not anymore. Haley dropped her chin and nestled against Ryan, letting his big body wrap around her as she drew comfort from his heartbeat and the heat of his skin.

"We've got to move. Finish your breakfast. I'll pack the gear."

He rose. She stared at a place somewhere in front of her as she thought of Maggie.

"Haley? Eat. We aren't stopping for lunch."

She lifted her oatmeal, stirring the congealed mess. Her appetite had fled with her sense of security. This man was as dangerous as wandering away from your friends on Bedford Avenue. She believed what he said but she needed to get away from him. His mission was not hers. Her mission was to get back home alive.

She choked down the oatmeal as Ryan deconstructed the tent and rolled their bedding. He had the packs ready before she had even finished washing her cup.

She followed Ryan through the forest for most of the morning until they emerged on a trail, marked with a yellow plastic disk nailed to the trunk of a tree.

"Is this the trail you wanted?" she asked.

"Pharaoh Mountain. Yes. We can take this to Graphite and from there follow the road to Lake George."

"I've been there! Big cold lake. The *Minne-Ha-Ha*, that's a paddle-wheeler, and mini golf. Oh, the town is cute, with ice-cream shops and nice stores."

Ryan was looking at her with an odd expression.

"They may have captured my courier. He may be in their hands right now. We aren't going mini golfing."

Haley nodded. "I'm sorry. I forgot."

"We may see hikers. So if we do, you and I are dating. I lost my shirt by hanging it over the fire to dry and it fell in."

"What about the bruises? All those abrasions?"

"I'll keep them under wraps. We are making a circular hike to the summit and then back to the Crane Pond parking lot."

"All right, Crane, like the bird."

"Yes. Your name is Anna Parker and I'm Don Gill."

"Unimaginative."

He adjusted his shoulder strap. She could only imagine how that heavy pack felt rubbing against his raw skin.

"The point is to be completely forgettable. No bright clothing, no interesting stories, just as dull as we can possibly be."

"That's no problem for me. But we're in trouble," she said.

"Why's that?"

She shook her head. "Any female who sees you is unlikely to forget."

His grin was wide enough to show dimples proving her point. Forgettable, Ryan Carr was not.

Chapter Nine

Haley did her level best, but even the flats were difficult for her with the heavy pack. He'd sprayed down her pack and her T-shirt in an effort to keep the blackflies from biting. Instead, they swarmed at a distance, coming in to bite and swerving away, repelled by the scent of the spray. She spent most of the morning either stumbling along or waving her hand before her face. In the sunny places the mosquitoes did not trouble her, but in the shade of the trees and the thick pine groves they seemed to lift from the forest floor and find any tiny place that bug spray had missed.

At noon they stopped at a spring to refill their water bottles and to scratch her bug bites. He instructed her to only drink from the water bottle through the filtering straw so as not to get any nasty little stomach bugs that would make her walk even more miserable. They ate the last of the granola bars and the fruit he had stolen from the cafeteria of the adventure camp.

Her shoulders throbbed. Her lower back ached. And she had never been so sweaty in her entire life.

But that wasn't quite true. She recalled hiking Lake

George with her father and mother and sister back when they were a family, complete and whole. She let her gaze wander about the clearing, catching glimpses of the lake through the trunks of the trees, and realized she'd missed being outdoors. Haley remembered a similar trip with Maggie, a day hike at Mount Marcy, the highest peak in New York State with the most amazing views.

She missed searching for the spotted orange salamanders she'd spied in the early spring along the way. Missed the soft loam of pine needles under her feet and the fresh, crisp snap of the air here. But she would never ever miss this backpack.

They continued on through the heat of the afternoon taking only one break for water.

"Ryan?"

He lowered the bottle and handed it to her, brows lifted.

"You were a Marine, right?"

He nodded, his expression going blank, but his eyes narrowing.

"Did you ever lose someone?"

Now his lips went bloodless and he stared off at the path before them, but she felt he was seeing something far away.

"I was a unit commander. And yes, I lost men, men who trusted me to keep them alive."

Men he cared about, clearly. So he understood loss. But instead of building a protective nest and crawling inside as she had, he took on the most dangerous missions possible.

"Drink," he ordered.

She did and then he retrieved the bottle, capping it with unnecessary force.

Why had he acted so differently? She puzzled over this as they set off again. Eventually she reached a logical conclusion. Haley grieved her sister, but did not feel responsible for her death because she wasn't a unit commander whose men trusted him to keep them alive. Ryan was experiencing survivor's guilt. She'd lay money on it, if she gambled. Which she didn't. Too risky.

The sounds of female voices brought Ryan to a stop. He flashed his dark eyes at her and reminded her that her name was Anna Parker. A moment later, a tall blonde woman appeared on the trail but her companion was not yet in view. The woman slowed at seeing Haley and Ryan. The second woman stepped out to peer at them. She had light brown skin and hair ironed straight. The rosy glow on her cheeks and the clear skin radiated good health. The perfectly applied liner made her eyes look golden and dramatic.

Both carried similar packs but unlike her they seemed to not notice the weight and moved gracefully along instead of using the rocking tread of a beast of burden that Haley had adopted sometime in the middle of the day. They called a greeting and then drew up before them.

"Heading for the summit?" the blonde one with the blue pack and the socks asked.

"Yes. That's the plan. We're going to climb to the summit and then camp at one of the lean-tos on the way back down. Then finish the climb tomorrow back at Crane Pond."

"We've been there and are just heading back," said the second woman.

Haley didn't like the looks of either of them. It wasn't just that they were cheerful or slim or athletic, though that was enough. It was something else, a niggling unease that she could not explain. She turned to Ryan.

"I'll just go use the little girls' room." She did not wait for his permission or response but spun away, leaving her pack and the three chatting about their hike. She moved behind the boulder that they had chosen to rest against. Moved deeper into the woods, making her way behind the two women. She watched them from her hiding place. And then she realized what it was that troubled her.

She and Ryan had spent only one night out in the woods and her hair was a mess. She wore no makeup. Her clothes were wrinkled and damp and she was quite certain she had circles under her eyes. But those two women looked like they had just stepped onto a movie set, one where they were pretending to be hikers. She studied their hair. She was willing to bet that both of them had a natural wave but their hair was ironed straight as dried linguine. Now, where would a woman plug in a straightening iron out here?

Haley selected a stout branch from the forest floor and crept forward. Perhaps she was wrong. But the insistent unease had grown, making her stomach clench as she made her way gingerly from one large tree trunk to the next.

RYAN WANTED TO be on their way, but Haley had not yet reappeared.

"Let me show you," said the brunette. She easily swung her pack down before her and reached for the side pocket, presumably to show him a map and the route that they had taken. But what he saw in her hand was no map. Her fingers wrapped around the grip of a pistol. She did not have time to draw it because he had her wrist captured and behind her back, dragging her before him as he relieved her of the gun.

When he lifted his gaze to her partner, it was to find she had her pistol out, arms extended, pointed at his chest in a stance that told him without words that she knew what she was doing.

"Where is it?" she asked.

"I'll kill her," Ryan warned, moving the pistol to her friend's temple.

The woman shrugged as if that threat was of no consequence. "Where is the flash drive, Mr. Carr?"

"I don't know what you're talking about."

She arched a sculpted brow and her crimson lips curled. "You told my colleagues that you knew where it was. But you left the job unfinished."

"My contact never delivered it," said Ryan.

"No?" She shook her head sadly. "We are quite sure Mr. Tanaka does not have it. So either you have it or you know where it is."

Ryan's stomach tightened. They knew Takashi's last name. His brows lowered as his frown deepened. "What did you do to him?"

"You should be worried about what I will do to you. Call your friend."

Ryan caught movement behind the blonde in his peripheral vision but did not redirect his gaze, maintaining eye contact. The woman in his arms struggled and tried to speak, tried to warn her friend. But Ryan tightened his hold on her throat and she went limp, choked out.

Behind the blonde, Haley wound back like a heavy hitter in a baseball lineup and swung her modified bat. The clunk of wood striking bone was sickening. The blonde's arms dropped slack to her sides as she sank to her knees and then fell forward to the ground. Ryan kicked the legs out from the woman he had captured. Then pressed a knee to the center of her back.

Haley stepped into the clearing, dropping the sturdy branch as she inched forward.

"Is she dead? Did I kill her?"

"Get her gun."

Haley stooped to check the woman's heart rate using two fingers at the base of her throat. Ryan wondered where she learned to do that.

"Still breathing," she said and sank back onto her heels, to blow away a breath as she squatted beside his attacker. "I thought I killed her," she whispered to herself.

"Gun," he said again. He glanced about listening for any approaching hikers.

This time Haley did as he asked, lifting the gun by the barrel and bringing it to him. He stuck it into the waistband of his cargo pants and then asked her to check inside the woman's pack.

"What am I looking for?" she asked.

He wasn't sure but he knew he would know when he saw it. From the side pockets came maps, a compass, a whistle knife and an extremely expensive tactical walkie-talkie.

"Keep looking," he said. The woman lying facedown under his knee roused and began to struggle. "Move again and you can join your friend."

The woman turned her head to see her blonde partner lying prone and limp, her face turned away. If he didn't know better, he'd think she was dead. She would be if Haley wasn't here. But killing was new to her and he was glad, even if it meant keeping these two killers alive.

The woman stilled as Haley searched through the pack.

"It's nearly empty. Just a baggie of food and something that looks like some kind of packing foam." She met his gaze. "I knew they hadn't been camping."

He cocked his head and wondered how she'd been able to perceive what he had not. At the bottom of the pack she found a kit. Inside was duct tape, rope, wire, zip ties and a black hood.

"What in the world?" she asked.

"Abduction kit. Bring it."

She did and he used the zip ties to secure the woman's wrists and ankles. Then he did the same to the unconscious woman. Finally, he pressed strips of tape across their mouths and dragged them both out of sight behind the boulder.

"You can't leave them here," Haley said.

"I am leaving them. I should kill them first."

"No," she said.

"That's the response I expected. You do know they were planning to kill you." He held up the single hood.

Haley swallowed, said nothing, but looked at the female agents.

"Don't worry," he said. "That one will be free before we make a quarter mile. But without weapons and her communication device, she'll need to return to base for new instructions."

Ryan searched the second woman's pack and came up with a similar radio, satellite phone and two mobile phones, all of which he would leave behind. He wasn't letting them track him with their equipment. But he wasn't letting them use them, either. He gathered the devices and methodically crushed each piece of electronics in between a rock and his boot heel.

Haley watched. "You know, you can keep the data from those phones and, without a power source, they can't track us."

He paused and glanced her way, boot raised. "Okay, do it."

Haley began collecting components from the shattered devices.

"Let me disable the rest," she said.

He stepped back. "Quickly. We need to get out of here."

He took a moment to rearrange their gear while Haley worked, offering her the hatchet. Then he left behind the cooking gear, two fuel cylinders, blankets, the tent, shovel and some of the food. He took the weapons, radios, water bottle filter system and the kit the women had packed. Then he shouldered the single pack.

"They were going to take me and call for backup. That means they're not alone. They have a recovery team nearby. Possibly a helicopter. That is the logical way to transport me out of this area. We have to make time. You ready?"

Haley gathered up the CPUs from the devices and he stowed them in a pocket of his cargo pants. Then she offered the hatchet.

"Leave it."

Ryan extended his hand and Haley took it. He set a brisk pace. How did she know about Takashi? Was that a bluff or had they captured and killed him? If his contact was dead, had he died before or after making the drop? He just didn't know. Possibly he was taking Haley into danger for no reason. He might very well reach the drop site and find nothing but more trouble.

EVEN WITHOUT A PACK, Haley was breathing hard as they climbed up the trail for Pharaoh Mountain. She read the sign and saw that they would ascend only 1,457 feet from the lake trail, but she never expected to do it at a near jog.

Ryan stopped twice. The first time was to refill their water containers and drink heavily through the blue plastic filtering straw designed to protect them from protozoa. Trotting along was bad enough. She could only imagine the added misery of digestive problems. His second stop was on top of the mountain.

"Those are the high peaks, the mountains with the highest elevation."

She had folded at the waist to suck much-needed oxygen into her lungs but straightened just enough to admire the blue vista. The view was magnificent. "You mean this isn't even a tall mountain?" she wheezed.

He gave a laugh.

"Uh-oh," he said, lifting the field glasses he had taken from the brunette's pack.

Haley didn't like the sound of that and straightened.

"We need to get off this rock and back under cover," he said, jogging away before she had a chance to ask why.

She glanced in the direction he had been looking, seeing nothing but a black speck. But then she heard it, the sound of a motor. Haley pinched her aching side and plunged after him.

"What is that?" she called.

"Helicopter. Our two hikers haven't checked in. That's probably their ride."

"We can't outrun a helicopter." Well, she couldn't, at least.

"Don't have to outrun it. Just have to get under the tree canopy where they can't spot us and hope they don't have infrared."

She was suddenly very glad that his backpack was a forest green rather than the bright blue and red carried by their attackers.

Ryan reached the tree line and stopped.

He glanced at her. "How did you know they were covert operatives?"

"I didn't. But I knew they weren't campers."

He cocked his head to the side. "They had all the right gear."

"I carried my pack for less than half a day and I was sweating so hard my shirt was sticking to my skin. My hairs were sticking to my face and if I was wearing any makeup it would be running down my cheeks in rivers. Meanwhile, they had time to apply their makeup, perfectly style their hair and shave their legs. Plus neither of them were sweating. They stood as if their packs weighed nothing at all, which was nearly the case."

"Huh. I'm paid to notice those sort of differences but I didn't see any of that."

"Perhaps that's why they sent two stunning women after you. I think I can guess what you did notice."

He had the good manners to flush at that. His embarrassment made him look even more charming. Haley gritted her teeth against the lure of this man. He was bad for her and might very well get her killed. The least she could do was not be yet another female to fall under his spell.

She pointed at the tree where the yellow marker was fixed above a blue one.

"Is that the trail we need?" she asked.

He glanced to the marker. "Yes. This one leads toward Graphite. From there we can take the road to Lake George."

"That's where you were supposed to get that package?"

"Yes, but if what they said is true, they found my contact already."

"What does that mean?" she asked. The disgruntle-ment was replaced with worry.

"It means they don't have the flash drive yet. That might be because Takashi escaped the initial ambush or because they are lying. Whether he made the drop is an open question. If he was captured after making the drop, he might have convinced them that I'm the one carrying it."

But if he did so, he'd be dead. Ryan was sure of that though he did not say so aloud.

"I told the three who took me that I had hidden it. That's why they didn't kill me. They believed I was tak-ing them to recover it."

"So your courier might be kidnapped. Or he might have escaped and be okay?"

Ryan's face was grim. "Come on. We need to go."

Chapter Ten

Ryan hoped they didn't have Takashi, that he had escaped or was dead. Either was preferable to capture.

Ryan hiked at a brisk pace on the descent. Behind him, Haley trotted along, keeping up with him as they tackled the steep trail. In some places this meant scrambling down over boulders. This route was not a beginning hike, as the signage had indicated.

Ryan glanced through the trees to the lake. He expected the female agents to be traveling with a tracker. The logical drop point would be Pharaoh Lake. From there the retrieval operation would have to hike to the summit to find the missing pair.

"What's that?" asked Haley.

He turned to see her pointing skyward. Ryan didn't see it yet but the prickling warning caused him to pluck Haley off the exposed rock face and run with her to the cover of the trees some fifteen yards away.

They reached the thick network of branches just before he heard the familiar thump of the chopper blades. He'd been wrong about the drop point.

"They're back."

As he watched from beneath the thick leafy canopy, two men fell backward from the open helicopter doors, one on each side. They repelled on cables straight down to the exposed rock surface of the summit. They would find the agents within minutes.

Ryan calculated the distance they had to travel and how far he could safely continue on the trail before they would need to leave it and bushwhack to make it more difficult for their pursuers to follow them.

"They're here for us. Right?" asked Haley.

"Yes." He grasped her shoulders and stared down at her beautiful flushed face. "Haley, those two men will be after us in a few minutes. The only way we avoid them is by hiding. I'm going to take us another mile down. Hopefully, get off the mountain. But then we're going to need to leave the trail. They don't have dogs so we may be able to elude them."

But that would depend on how good those men were at tracking.

"There's only two of them. Same as us."

He shook his head. "That's just the vanguard. They'll have agents spread out throughout the trail, coming from the top and from the bottom."

"Who are they?"

"I'm not sure I'll ever know. The intel we collected is Chinese. I'll try to explain later. Have to go."

Ryan knew they had made the right decision reducing his pack to the bare essentials needed for survival. Now he could scramble over rocks when he had to. Haley trailed behind and he paused to wait for her. Her legs were becoming clumsy. She couldn't keep up this pace much longer. But he had to admire her for sticking with him this long. He could, of course, leave her behind. Should, in fact. But he found the thought brought him physical pain. How had he become so attached to her so quickly?

He couldn't remember the last time he had been even vaguely attached to anyone or anything. The supervisor said it was what made him so perfect for these assignments. This apparent detachment from danger. He wasn't reckless on the job, just fearless. The shrinks said it stemmed from his father's death. Ryan didn't know or care. It made him an asset and that was what mattered.

"Not much farther and we can rest."

He led them along to the place where the mountain trail intersected the lake trail. He paused to listen. How far behind them were their pursuers? He didn't know but the time pressed heavily upon them.

"Orange trail," said Haley. "Where does that go?"

"That's our trail, but we can't take it. I have to see if those two are on us. We'll leave this one at the stream."

"Voices," hissed Haley, hunching and pointing to the lake trail.

There was no time to run, so Ryan led them from the trail and into the forest of white birch and maple. He sank down at the base of a large oak and pulled Haley down beside him.

From his position low to the ground he watched two hikers with day packs. One male, one female. The woman was chattering away as they paused at the junction of the yellow and orange trails.

"Love to summit," said the young man. "But no time

on a day hike." He was blond with a bushy brown beard and a bandanna tied across his forehead to absorb the sweat. He wore an athletic T-shirt with a plaid flannel shirt tied around his waist. Shorts, woolen socks and well-worn hiking boots finished his outfit.

"Next trip," said the small brunette. She looked fit and young, with long tanned legs that stretched beneath short shorts. She adjusted her day pack and looked in the direction that Haley and Ryan had just come. She smiled and lifted a hand to someone Ryan could not see.

"Hey there," she called.

The sound of automatic weapon gunfire caused Haley to gasp and then press both hands over her mouth.

The two hikers fell back as if knocked to the ground by a strong wind. Ryan could no longer see them but he did see the two men dressed in combat fatigues carrying semiautomatic rifles.

He glanced at Haley to see her hand still pressed tight over her mouth. Above her clenching fingers her nostrils flared and her eyes went wide with shock.

Ryan watched as the men crept forward, weapons raised.

The first said, "One male. One female."

The second said, "Yellow. His hair isn't yellow."

What followed was very colorful cursing. "Not them. Keep going."

The two men flipped their rifles mechanically to their backs and continued along the ascending summit trail. Their footfalls were heavy as the two men jogged away from this position. The stillness was broken only by the wind moving through the leaves above them. The next sound they heard was the harsh cry of a jay farther down the trail. The men had reached a bird, who called a warning to the forest. A red squirrel rustled the leaves below the maple to their left. Then, spotting them, it scrambled up the trunk and out of sight.

Ryan shifted so that his mouth was pressed to Haley's ear.

"We have to move."

She lowered her trembling hand from her mouth. Her words came in frantic little pants as she struggled to breathe past the horror.

"They thought they were us."

Ryan nodded as he sat up and pulled her beneath one arm. Her entire body shook.

"They just shot them down. Like the men in the cabin and those women. They want to kill us."

"Easy to search a dead man."

Haley stared toward the two fallen hikers.

"They were just having a hike. They aren't even a part of this."

Wrong place, wrong time, Ryan thought but said nothing as he rubbed her back in wide circles.

"Breathe," he whispered.

"Should we go and check them? Be sure that they're…"

No, he thought. The two females might be behind them.

But he said, "Yes. I'll check."

And he did, but not for the reason she thought.

"Will they just shoot anyone they meet?" Haley's voice now held a note of indignation. "Just kill them because they happen to be on the same trail where we might be?"

She looked away from him and stood up. He was certain she could now see at least some part of the two bodies on the trail. He watched as her hands curled into fists.

"This isn't right. Before I was just trying to survive. But now I want those two killers caught and punished. I want to get that information to our government."

Ryan saw the determination in her stance and the white in her knuckles. Haley was no longer afraid. Now she was furious. She turned to him, eyes flashing. He thought he'd never seen a more stirring sight.

"Let's go," she said, chin high and gaze cold as cut crystal. "We have to find your friend and get that flash drive."

Chapter Eleven

Ryan nodded and stood. Haley was no longer running for her life. Now she was running to help him complete his mission. It was something he could never have predicted from the shy, timid little female who rescued him from the road.

But she did look both determined and fierce, not at all the female he had met only a day ago.

"Wait here." He left her to move from cover to the trail. There, he checked the two, finding them both dead. Then he released the knot from the shirt tied about the man's hips and dragged the garment from the corpse. By the time he'd returned to her, he had shed his blanket poncho and shrugged into the flannel. This would make him far less memorable to anyone who might see them. Then he shouldered his pack and consulted his compass, picking his direction, aiming for the stream he knew ran in the direction of Lake George and the town of Graphite.

They moved swiftly and as quietly as possible, reaching the stream in less than two miles. From there it was only a matter of scrambling along the bank, keeping parallel to the shore until they reached an improved, graded dirt road. Ryan chose not to move from cover but to remain in the woods. He kept the road in sight and the going was slower. When a chopper swept low over the trees, he knew he'd made the right call.

"Same one?" she asked.

He paused to glance upward. "Yes."

Ryan handed her the water bottle and she drank thirstily. He took a few swallows and then tucked the nearly empty bottle into the pack. A fenced gravel pit was the first sign of civilization. There were no structures within the fencing, so he continued on. They made their way around an occupied cabin, judging from the curl of wood smoke. They passed a double-wide trailer surrounded by yard ornaments and hummingbird feeders buzzing with the jewel-colored creatures.

Haley was stumbling along now, past exhausted. Her fury had ebbed and now she rocked wearily on her feet like a prize fighter whose body has not yet realized it has been knocked out.

Dusk stole the colors from the day. Ryan knew that soon he'd have to make a decision on a place to bed down.

With the sun now well behind the ridgeline, Ryan risked moving to the road. Helicopters did not often fly at night and unless they had thermal imaging, he and Haley would be invisible in the darkness.

He slowed his pace again as Haley's tread grew more clumsy. She needed rest and he needed to find a place where they could sleep in safety. The opportunity came three-quarters of a mile down the road.

There he found a ranch-style home. Behind the drawn curtains, the front window glowed with the flickering blue light of a large television. Beside the house in the wide drive were a collection of vehicles. There was a pickup truck, an older-model Dodge Caravan and a small economy car. Beside this and off the drive was a trailer holding a small motorboat that was draped with a fitted blue vinyl cover. Beside that was a Coachmen travel trailer.

It was the sort of RV that one hauls with a pickup truck. He judged it to be about twenty-one feet in length and exceedingly easy to break into.

"Wait here."

She clutched his arm. "Why?"

"I just need to scout the area and be certain that we can get out of here if we need to."

Haley waited with his pack as he circled the house. He found no evidence of a dog. From the back deck, he had a clear view through the kitchen window into the living room at the front of the small house. There were two people, middle-aged, one male and one female, sitting in overstuffed chairs watching the television with faces slack and eyes vacant. The bedrooms were all illuminated so he guessed there might be two teenagers in the house. This was only a guess from the age of the couple and the number of autos the family had collected, and the lights. He circled the garage and found that it overflowed with a collection of both useful and discarded household gear. Behind the garage was a shed and beyond was a wide yard that dipped down to the stream. Past that, the forest stood dark against the rising moon.

He returned to Haley and together they made it to the camper. As it turned out, he didn't even have to break in because the door was unlocked.

Haley quietly mounted the stairs and then stopped on the linoleum just inside before the dinette and kitchen area. He dropped his pack at the top of the stairs and opened the blinds on the opposite side of the camper, above the combo sink and stove. Moonlight filtered into the space, showing a living area with sleeper sofa and lounge chairs in the forward section.

In the opposite direction, the trailer narrowed to a corridor leading to what he assumed would be a cramped bathroom and a bedroom beyond.

"Are we staying here?" she asked.

"Yes. I'll fix us some supper and then we can rest for a few hours. We need to be up and out before they are," he said, thumbing toward the house.

"What if they come out here?"

He shook his head. "They won't. They're in for the night. No reason to come out here unless they see a light or hear something."

Ryan moved to open the kitchen window and then the one on the opposite side. The fresh air filtered through the trailer, gradually removing the stale odor within.

Instead of using his supplies, he checked the camper cabinets and found no food but a completely stocked kitchen including dishes, pots, pans, utensils and several cans of Sterno. So he used a borrowed pot and Sterno to cook a double serving of beef Stroganoff. They sat side by side at the narrow dinette shoveling the food into their mouths. He felt the lift of the food reaching his stomach and the sustenance surging into his body, giving it energy.

They ate from a single pot. Afterward they tried the dehydrated ice cream, which he found crunchy and weird.

"Sticks to my teeth," she said. "But it's sweet."

He nodded.

"Ryan, is this normal for you?"

"What?"

"Running from helicopters, watching people killed right in front of you?"

"Every operation is different."

"Do you like this work?"

"It's important."

She went quiet, thinking, he supposed. Finally, she asked, "What prepares you for this? What I mean is, what did you do before you were a spy?"

"Operative."

"Hmm?"

"We're called operatives or agents. Not spies. I was a soldier," he said. "Marines. The Company recruited me from there. I'm good at blending in."

"Do you have a wife or girlfriend?"

"Not anymore."

"Hmm," she said, thoughtful again. "What about family?"

"Aunts, uncles, cousins. My mom and dad died when I was young."

She shifted in the seat so she faced him. "How young?"

He watched her as he spoke. "Twelve."

She flinched. "What happened? An accident?"

"No. They were older when they had me. Mom was forty-three and dad was forty-eight when I was born. My dad was diagnosed with liver cancer when he turned sixty. It was everywhere by the time he had symptoms. My mom died eleven days after he did. Undiagnosed heart condition, they said. Worn out taking care of my dad. That's what my aunt Deanna said."

Haley said nothing for a time, just watched him with her shimmering pale eyes. The silence growing heavy, pressing down on him.

"I'm sorry," she said at last.

He said nothing to this.

"Who took care of you? Afterward, I mean."

"My father's younger sister. That's what was in his will. My grandfather was appointed to handle the money because my dad didn't trust his sister not to spend it on her kids. She had eight. But then Gramps was dead before my parents so that didn't work out as planned. There was nothing left for school so I joined up. Best move I ever made."

"Why do you say so?"

"Because it gave me a purpose."

"What purpose?"

"To protect this country."

"Is that why you do this?"

His nod was mechanical. She narrowed her eyes on him as if she did not quite buy what he was selling. How had she sensed the half-truth?

His stomach squeezed and his breath grew shallow.

He lifted his chin against the challenge in her gaze. "Hey, I like a challenge. I've hiked Everest. I've surfed in New Zealand. I've jumped out of airplanes more times than I can remember and I've swum with hammerhead sharks in Australia."

"You seem like you're tempting fate."

"Just letting her know I'm not afraid."

"Hmm," she said again. "I try to avoid unnecessary risks."

"Seems like you avoid the necessary ones, as well."

"Better than being so cavalier with your life."

He shrugged. "If you say so."

Her voice took on a defensive edge. "It would kill my parents if anything happened to me."

"Not living is maybe worse than dying, Haley."

"I'm living."

"Really. Living in your sister's apartment. Hiding from people and experiences." He shook his head. "Be honest, can you really say your life is what you want it to be?"

"Currently, no."

"Will you go back to your old life after what we've been through?" he asked.

"Just as fast as I can. If I live through this, I plan to lie to my parents and tell them that I had a wonderful time at adventure camp."

"You have a boyfriend?"

"We were talking about you."

"Were we?"

"I asked if you had a wife or girlfriend and you said, 'Not anymore.' Were you married?"

"Almost. I was engaged when I joined the service. Katie was pretty, smart, too smart to wait around for me."

"She broke it off?"

"She did. You know what my first response was?"

Haley shook her head.

"Relief. We got along fine and that seemed a poor reason to get engaged and a worse one to get married. I should have told her that, instead of putting her off."

"You aren't optimistic enough."

"What's that?"

"Optimistic enough to be married. It requires faith in the future and in another person."

He nodded. "That's right. And a wife is a liability. Someone who could be used against me. And I couldn't share what I do with her. I'm allowed to tell a wife what I do, but I wouldn't. It would worry her too much. Katie would have freaked. Insisted I quit and get a job with her father. He leases commercial buildings. Can you imagine? I'd die all right, but it would be of boredom."

He chuckled and turned to see her reaction. He found Haley sagging in the dinette. Her eyelids drooped and her chin sank to her chest. He placed a hand on her shoulder and gave a squeeze. Her head snapped up and her eyes blinked open.

"Would you like the bedroom or the sofa?"

"What?" she glanced about and then seemed to remember where she was. "Oh, I want the bed, but I don't want to be in there alone." She looked up at him with wide innocent eyes.

Adventure camp, he thought. Sleeping beside her

might give her the kind of adventure she'd never planned on. As if she could have anticipated any of this.

He knew she wasn't coming on to him, but it didn't matter to his body. The surging of energy and blood moved south and he shifted uncomfortably.

"I don't think that is such a great idea."

Her eyes widened in understanding. "Oh, well, then you can take the bed. I'll just sleep, uh, here?"

He snorted and then set about stowing the nearly empty Sterno can. Then he wiped the empty pot and packed it and two unopened Sterno cans with his gear. He'd clean it when and if the opportunity presented itself.

Then he extended his hand. "Come on."

She laced her fingers though his and he led her to the bedroom. The mattress was bare. He left her to retrieve his pack, pulling out the poncho blanket before retracing his steps.

When he reached the bedroom, it was to find Haley had stripped out of her jeans. Her bra sat on the crumpled denim beside her boots. Haley lay curled on her side on the mattress, hugging a decorative pillow, dressed in socks, underwear and her jacket. Even in the blue moonlight filtering through the blinds, he knew it was a picture he'd not soon forget.

He draped the poncho blanket over her. She sighed and nestled into the mattress.

Then he sat on the bed and tugged off his boots. He remained dressed in his cargo pants and the borrowed flannel. It was little protection against the desire he held for her, but it would have to be enough. Fatigue tugged at his sore muscles and healing wounds.

Ryan slipped beneath the coverings and Haley nestled up against him, seeking his warmth, he told himself. He tucked her close to his chest and rested his chin on the top of her head. He could get used to this.

He closed his eyes and allowed himself to rest, dragged down into sleep like a creature caught in a vortex.

He woke in the darkness to feel her moving. Her breathing had changed and her hand was splayed over his stomach. She'd threaded her palm under the hem of his shirt so that skin contacted skin.

"Haley?" he murmured. "What's wrong?"

"I don't know. Just woke up."

"Sleep while you can."

She lay her head on the crook of her arm and then shifted, restlessly.

"What?"

"I have to pee."

"We best go outside," he said.

She slipped into her jeans and boots as he dragged on his boots. He headed outside into the chill. The wet grass clung to his legs as he led her behind the garage. Then he left her and continued on to the shed.

He was just finishing when he heard the engine and then the crunch of tires on gravel. He crept back to Haley to find her peering around the corner of the garage.

"Someone just pulled in," she said.

The cab door of the SUV opened, illuminating a

young man who paused to retrieve his hat from the seat beside him. He knew that headgear. The hat looked exactly like the ones worn by Smokey the Bear except for the purple ribbon.

"State police," he said. "Wait here. I've got to get my pack."

The young man stood and adjusted his utility belt. Then he headed for the house.

"He'll see you," she warned, holding his hand.

The trooper moved out of his line of sight, heading for the front door.

"If he goes into the house, I can get back to the trailer."

"But how will you get out?"

"Haley, they'll know we were there and the bed is probably still warm. We won't get far on foot once they have our position."

She released him and he slipped out of cover and to the RV. He reached the entrance as the front door to the house opened. The trooper was speaking to someone. Ryan slipped inside the trailer and dashed to the bedroom, whisking the blanket from the bed. Then he retraced his steps, glad that his pack was ready and he had left no traces of their occupancy. He shouldered the pack and then turned to the open windows. He had the one by the dinette closed and was moving to the one above the sink. He closed it as the trooper returned down the walkway, his flashlight out and the beam shining along the path to the driveway and then lifting to the mobile home.

He was trapped.

Chapter Twelve

Haley crept along the garage's exterior wall, the wide rough planks flaking old paint as she went. From here she could see the state trooper heading from the ranch-style house to the mobile home. The wide beam of the flashlight illuminated the path before the young officer. She glanced back toward the wood line. She knew she could make it there but feared for both Ryan and the trooper. She could not stand the idea of anything happening to the young man or Ryan being arrested by the trooper.

She crept toward the trailer, unsure what to do.

Something scurried inside the garage. She froze in place and flattened against the wall. A large waddling mammal appeared from the open garage door. She recognized the gray body and ringed tail identifying the creature as a raccoon. She stepped toward the garage door opening as the plan flashed fully formed before her. The creature spotted her and trotted in the opposite direction down the driveway. Haley grasped the large plastic garbage bin and tossed it to its side. Then she darted out of sight along the outer wall of the garage.

The flashlight beam swung in her direction. She crouched along the exterior of the building. She pressed her hand to her mouth, her body trembling as she waited in the cold night air. If she ran he might hear her. The crunch of gravel accompanied his footsteps in her direction.

"Shoo! Get out of here, you."

The raccoon appeared in the beam of his flashlight as it moved perpendicular to both her and the trooper's position. In a moment the officer vanished from the mown lawn into the tall grass bordering the driveway.

The crunch of approaching footsteps grew louder. She recognized the sound of the garbage bin being righted. The trooper continued inside the garage. His flashlight beam shone through the dirty side window as the front door of the camper opened and Ryan descended. On his back was the single pack he carried. He carefully closed the door behind him and glanced about. She did not stand or give away her position but tracked him as he moved in a course parallel to the raccoon vanishing into the tall grass. Haley crept away from the garage, following Ryan. She continued through the field, pausing only when she was far enough from the buildings to be hidden in the tall weeds. There, she waited, listening. The beam of the flashlight moved from her position. She lifted her head like a gopher from the grass to find the trooper's light now shining through the window of a garden shed that she had not known was there. She ducked as the trooper emerged and flashed his light in her direction.

She lay flat, holding one hand over her heart now

crashing against her ribs. Several minutes later she heard his heels crushing the gravel again and then caught the familiar click and squeak of the screen door to the camper. Would he see any evidence of their occupancy?

The grass was wet and she began to shiver as she waited an eternity for the sound of the trooper returning to the house. Then she recalled that wet grass left a definite trail and worried he might see the flattened blades or the silver trail of her footsteps on the shorter grass now covered with dew. The grass had been wet enough to soak her soaks and bare legs.

She stared up watching gray clouds sweeping along the dark sky but realized she could not see stars. That meant that dawn was coming. Which direction was east?

She had no idea, which reminded her again that she had no business playing secret agent with the real McCoy.

At last came the engine of his cruiser turning over before the officer finally backed his vehicle out of the drive.

She waited one minute. Two. And then the third. Finally, she stood up to find Ryan doing the same, his position a mere twenty-five feet from hers. She ran the distance that separated them, wet goldenrod and weeds lashing her legs. Then she threw herself into his open arms. He pulled her close.

She pressed against the hard planes of his chest, her breathing rapid. Sweet relief flooded through her as she looked up into his rugged bearded face.

Ryan inclined his head and she had time for a swift inhale of air before his mouth pressed to hers. The kiss was hard and demanding. She whimpered and opened her lips at his insistence.

Now her heart pounded for a different reason. Her skin flushed and her body quickened. She wrapped her arms about his neck and dragged him closer, urging him to deepen the kiss.

This was a bad idea. She slipped her tongue along his with quick darting thrusts. What was she doing? The hot rush of need chased away the cold.

At last he pulled back, looking at her as if she had become a complete stranger. He shook his head as if to clear it.

"Haley?" he said, as if unsure it was her.

"I'm sorry. I got carried away."

"It's all right with me. But…" He still gazed at her as if she were a live grenade.

"You kissed me first."

"I did. I did." Was he trying to convince himself? "Never expected…"

"What?"

"Nothing. I'm just glad to see you. Lucky he went for the garage first. That 'coon knocked over a bin."

"*I* knocked over the bin just as soon as I saw the raccoon."

"You did that?"

She nodded.

"That was fast thinking." He lifted a hand to stroke her cheek, his fingers lingering on her neck as he stared down at her. His mouth opened as if he might say something else.

"You really aren't what I expected."

She lifted her brow in question and then turned her head to press her cheek to his palm, longing for the heat and rough scratch of his calluses on her sensitive skin.

"I want to kiss you."

"You just did."

"That was relief. This one is something else."

"What?"

"Not really sure. I thought, I just felt…" He pressed his mouth into a stingy line.

She smiled and stepped closer, placing her hands on his shoulders.

He kissed her again. This time his mouth was gentle, a sweet promise. The purr of longing rumbled from her throat. Her hands went under his shirt, caressing the smooth skin and taut muscle. He trembled in response and leaned in, pressing his hips to hers. She rubbed against him and he gasped.

Ryan set her at arm's length.

"You know we still might not survive this."

"I'm aware."

"And if we do, I'll be leaving you to deliver this intel."

"Ryan, you gave me a kiss. Not an engagement ring."

He nodded and then exhaled. Then he lifted the pack that lay beside him in the tall grass.

"I just don't usually kiss women like you. Most of the females I associate with are either operatives or women who are not looking for long-term company."

His insistence to put her into a category annoyed her. He had her all figured out, did he? Knew exactly the type of man she would prefer and exactly the sort of relationship she would insist upon?

"It may interest you to know that I am also not interested in long-term relationships. Nor marriage. Nor raising a family. I enjoy my work, my friends and my own company."

Now his brows lifted.

"Surprised?"

He nodded. "Why no children?"

It was none of his business, really.

"Which direction shall we head now?" Haley looked from one direction to the next.

"We have to make it to Lake George. I'd love to steal one of those cars, but chances are good they would hear it and us."

"There's a bike in the garage." Haley pointed back in the direction they had come.

"The bicycle would be too hard to navigate on these gravel roads. And it is at least four miles to the lake and another six to the town of Lake George."

"Well then, it's a good thing that it's a motorcycle and not a bicycle."

Ryan smiled and led the way back to the garage. It wasn't exactly a motorcycle. More a motorbike, the kind a young man would use on a dirt track or private property. It even had a number fixed to the front between the handlebars.

"This is great," said Ryan. "I can roll it far enough away from the house that they won't hear me hot-wiring the engine. Plus it's a simple enough motor to jump and if we see or hear anyone else, this bike will be easy to put out of sight." Ryan rocked the bike back and forth and heard the sloshing gasoline in the tank. He took the time necessary to locate a gas can and fill the tank before rolling the bike down the drive to the road. He walked beside the bike and she flanked the opposite side. They continued until the house was no longer in sight and then farther still. A mile, she thought, or darn close. It was hard to judge distances in the dark, she realized.

"I think the motor might be pretty loud on this one. I see the tailpipe is rusted and it's very likely going to roar once I get it started."

"What time do you think it is?"

"Early. Maybe four a.m. See?" He pointed ahead of them to the sky. "Stars are fading and the sky is turning dark blue. Won't be long before you can see bands of sunlight coming up in the eastern sky."

She turned to look at the ridgeline, a dark silhouette against the sky, and he laughed.

"That way." He pointed in the opposite direction.

Ryan stopped and asked her to hold the bike, which had no kickstand. He fiddled in the darkness and she wondered how he could see what he was doing.

Suddenly the motor turned over with a growl. He twisted one of the handles and the motor coughed and then roared. She saw the flash of his teeth.

"No room for the pack. Just give me a minute to get what we need."

He left nearly everything except the weapons, including the pistols he had taken from their attackers at Schroon Lake. He clipped the water bottle to his belt and stowed the guns in the various pockets of his cargo pants.

"Can you carry these?" He offered the last of the snack packs.

She put them in her coat with her multi-tool and waited while he swung a leg over the small bike.

"Climb on," he said. He looked enormous on the tiny bike.

"Isn't this bike designed for one?"

"I guess it is, so you better hold tight." He scooted as far forward as his body would allow, keeping one foot on the ground to steady the bike as she gingerly climbed up behind him.

Half her backside was off the rear of the seat. She wrapped her arms about his middle and squeezed tight. She felt the rumble of his laugh as he pushed off. She could see nothing over his wide shoulders. How he managed to navigate the graded road in the darkness, she could not say.

Both the lack of light and her lack of view made it seem as though they were rocketing along at great speeds. However, she was fairly certain that a bike such as this could not go more than about fifty miles an hour.

She saw evidence of other houses and felt the bump as they left the gravel and continued on pavement. When the engine slowed to an idle and he set his foot down she lifted her head.

"Climb off."

She did, and followed him as he left the road for the wide shoulder that was in need of mowing. He rolled the bike down a short incline on the graded hill that allowed water to run off the highway and gave them an easy hiding place. There in the ditch he set the bike on its side. She watched the headlights approaching.

"Down," he said.

They lay side by side as the vehicle moved past them and continued on its way. He waited until there was no sound before returning to the road. This same process was repeated three more times as the sky turned pink and then orange.

Once underway again, she watched the sun's rays touch the very tops of the tall pines at the ridge beside the road, gilding the needles. Sunrise, she realized, which meant it was about six in the morning. By the time they reached the road that flanked Lake George, the sun was well up.

Though not among New York State's Finger Lakes, Lake George was narrow and deep, and also carved by a glacier. The result was a long, beautiful body of water running north to south and stretching from the village of Lake George to Ticonderoga beside the southernmost tip of Lake Champlain.

The fort once held the English territory against the French in the French and Indian War and was a reconstruction, she believed. She and her father had toured the historic site and watched the reenactors shoot off the cannons.

She smiled at the memory.

"We need a new set of wheels," he shouted back at her.

Numerous cabins and lake houses lined the steep

banks of the western shore of the lake. Ryan slowed several times as she admired how the water of the lake reflected the bright blue sky. It was going to be another clear day, she realized.

Finally, Ryan found what he sought, a late-model RAM pickup with rusted-out rear fenders and filled with a load of firewood heaped in disarray.

It was a good choice, she thought, easily overlooked and forgettable.

Haley held the bike as he worked under the console of the truck. She craned her neck at the house, expecting someone to emerge at any moment.

By the time the truck motor turned over, she was certain the family in that lake house would hear them. But despite appearances, the motor purred like new. Ryan returned to her and took the motorbike, secreting it behind the woodpile, and then opened the truck's passenger door for her.

Once underway she glanced at the dash and saw it was nearly ten in the morning.

"Where are you supposed to meet the courier?"

"Not meet. I'll be checking a dead drop."

"What's a dead drop?"

"It's a predetermined place for your contact to leave information that will not be accidentally discovered. It takes two agents to make an exchange without meeting in person. We use wireless drops now. We can transmit data from a handheld device just by getting close to it. But this drop is old-school. If Takashi made it, I just need to pick it up. He carried the intel over the Canadian border and I take it from here."

"Why?"

He paused and she remembered what he'd said about telling her nothing other than what she already knew. Ryan rubbed his neck, thinking.

"You've risked your life to help me."

She nodded because that was true.

"My courier's name is Takashi. He's a foreign operative who has dual citizenship, US and Japanese. He is currently working with the Company from China, an ally, but that doesn't make him welcome at headquarters."

"What company?"

Ryan's mouth quirked. "The Company is what we call the CIA."

Her eyes widened but she nodded her understanding. "I thought you said he was a Japanese intelligence agent."

"He is."

"But you said…" She gasped. "A double agent!"

"Shh," he said. "He's no double agent. He works for the Japanese government. His people felt this intel needed to be with us. He delivered it."

She covered her mouth and hunched. "Sorry," she whispered. "Do you know where this information has come from?"

"I know where we believe it to have originated."

"Will you tell me?"

He glanced at her then returned his focus to the road. "Haley, the less you know the better."

"I have never found that to be true."

"We're here. They'll be looking for both of us together so I need you to stay in the truck."

She planned to do just that, at least until he was out of sight.

Chapter Thirteen

Haley watched Ryan walk along the street that faced the lake. The tourist area had changed little since she had seen it last. There was the ice-cream shop where her dad would buy his daughters sundaes that neither of them could finish and right next door the candy shop where they would buy saltwater taffy for his younger sister. A gift that Haley later learned that her aunt loathed because the sticky taffy pulled at her dental work.

Ryan continued past the T-shirt shop, skirting around the family sticking their heads through the cutouts of nineteenth-century passengers preparing to board the paddle wheeler.

There, he crossed the street, heading toward the dock that stretched out over the water, offering slips for various boats, and led, she remembered, to the paddle wheeler, *Minne-Ha-Ha*.

Was he planning to go on board?

Haley thought this her best chance to check on her parents, so she slipped out of the vehicle and headed in the opposite direction. She did not know where the police station might be, but remembered that there was always lots of police presence in the tourist area. The town was careful about protecting its most reliable source of income.

She passed the ice-cream shop pausing only to glance through the window, past the ornate gold lettering, to the table where she had sat with her family back in the time when they were whole and complete. Before Maggie's death tore the family in half. A new family now sat there, happy with their treats and with time to do as they pleased. She looked at the children, a girl and young boy, and hoped they'd fare better than she and her sister, Maggie.

"I love ice cream. Don't you?"

Haley startled.

"Sorry!" said the unfamiliar male voice. "I startled you."

Her smile was automatic as she regarded him, judging the man to be of college age. He wore a T-shirt advertising a band that she was vaguely aware of and Jams shorts. His sneakers were unlaced with the ends tucked into the shoe. His face was lean and his mirror sunglasses disguised his eyes.

"They pipe the smell of the caramel corn and fudge out here in the street." He smiled and pointed at the vent between the awning and window. "It's a killer later in the day."

She smiled. "I remember."

"Can I buy you a cone?" He pointed to entrance. "Can I buy you a cup?"

She hesitated. "Um, you know, I'd like that, but

would you mind me borrowing your phone? I left mine in my hotel room."

"Oh? Sure." He handed it over, smiling brightly, hoping to buy her an ice cream. Really, she should tell him to run in the opposite direction and keep running until he lost sight of her.

"Thanks." She accepted the phone and paused before dialing. Calling her father was risky. They might be tracking all calls to his number. But this stranger didn't know her father. Was she dragging him into this mess in the same way that she'd been ensnared? If they traced this call, they might find out where they were.

"What's wrong?" asked the young man.

She forced a smile. "Nothing. Just trying to remember the number."

Not knowing if her parents were safe from all this was tearing her up. She gritted her teeth and dialed her father.

The phone rang only once before connecting.

"Hello?" said her dad, cautious as he prepared for a telemarketer.

"Dad?"

"Haley? Is that you?"

"Hi, Dad!" she was laughing now, relief mingling with a sense of normalcy.

"Everything okay? I didn't think you could use your phone."

"Well, I'm borrowing one."

"Oh, is everything okay?"

She sniffed. "Fine."

He must have heard the strain in her voice. "Haley,

if you really hate it, you can come home. I'll think of something to tell your mom. I'm just sorry that she was right again. I really thought you might like it."

Adventure camp. He thought she was upset by adventure camp.

"No, I'm fine. I just wanted to hear your voice."

"Ah, honey."

"I've got to…run… I have a…a class in a few minutes."

"What class?" He sounded excited now.

She smiled. "It's like orienteering."

"Oh, like a treasure hunt? What's that called, geocaching. Right?"

"Sort of."

"That sounds great. Just great!" He was overemphasizing again, as he did when trying to coax her into joining something. This time she had. She'd joined something bigger than herself.

"It is great. I love you, Dad. Please tell Mom the same from me."

"Sure, honey. I love you, too."

The silence stretched. Now he'd say, *Bye, honey, I'm hanging up now.* Then he'd lower the phone gently back to the cradle and she'd hear that familiar clunk. She waited and then thought of him, at home, worried that she might not be quite all right and wondering if he should hang up or continue to reassure.

"Um, bye, Dad." Haley disconnected. She handed back the phone to the young man. "Thanks very much."

She spotted the police officer who was now moving in her direction, his eyes fixed upon her.

"Haley Nobel?" he asked.

"Yes."

Why had she said yes. She turned to face him. The officer's hands went to his sides, to the gun and the radio.

"I need you to turn around," he said.

The young man was gawking at her, clearly speechless.

She did and then she leaped over the park bench and ran. Behind her the officer shouted. She had two advantages: she was a regular at her gym in Brooklyn and the officer was carrying about fifty pounds of gear. He, however, had a mobile police force, which he was likely calling. She glanced back and saw he had opted for his radio. The hunt was on.

RYAN WALKED PAST the six-and-a-half-foot Frankenstein who wore full makeup right down to his elevator shoes. The employee of the House of Horrors wax museum posed with two tourists while a third took the photo on her phone. Beyond the museum, the adjoining building jutted out an additional three feet before the shops continued. Along that blank stretch of wall sat a blue soda vending machine. Ryan leaned against the wall. Frankenstein did a great job of distracting the crowds of vacationers from him as Ryan slipped his arm into the gap between the vending machine and the brick wall.

At first he felt nothing, and his heart sank. Dead end, he thought. All for nothing.

Then he swept his hand slightly lower and felt adhesive tape. Takashi was several inches shorter than him.

He'd extended his arm and placed the drop just slightly below a comfortable sweep of Ryan's arm.

He stooped as he pried the corner of the tape away until he removed the envelope with the gray duct tape still clinging to the front.

"Bingo!" he whispered and tipped the envelope, disappointed that no flash drive fell into his palm. He withdrew the folded page.

At that moment he heard someone shouting.

"Hey, stop!"

Frankenstein and the tourists all swiveled their heads in the direction of the commotion. He slipped the envelope into the pocket of the garment he had taken from the murdered hiker and a sinking feeling pinned him in place.

She hadn't stayed in the truck.

He just had time to tug down the zipper of the pocket when Haley dashed into view, long legs pumping and arms swinging as she ran. She did not look behind her at the police officer in pursuit. He was falling behind and, perhaps seeing the folly of continuing on foot, slowed and lifted his radio.

Haley dashed by and Ryan lifted the hood of his jacket as he pushed off the wall and ambled after the two. The officer slowed as Haley darted down an alley. The officer continued at a lope down the narrow passage where she had vanished and then turned back to the street. Ryan knew he should return to the truck, deliver the package left by his courier and forget he'd ever met Haley Nobel.

An image of her face peering down at him from her

car as he lay bleeding in the road flashed in his mind. She'd saved him and she'd attacked one of the two female agents who'd gotten the drop on him and she'd distracted the trooper so he could escape the mobile home.

He owed her. Big-time.

But that didn't supplant his orders.

The pursuit offered a wonderful distraction. He should leave her.

Instead, he trailed them to the back of the row of shops and the wide expanse of the parking lot beyond. Haley disappeared behind a row of vehicles and ducked out of sight.

From somewhere far too close came the sound of sirens. The village of Lake George was responding to the call for backup. If they took her into custody, it would be one less distraction. But he knew that the first to respond to the news of her arrest would not be DEA officers. Once they took her, there was little to no chance of getting her back. And he wanted her back, badly enough to risk his mission. He darted out into the parking area. The police officer never saw him as he ran parallel to his course. Once he reached the row where Haley disappeared, he dropped and scanned for her legs. Seeing nothing, he moved forward and repeated his efforts. On the sixth try he saw her wet boots and muddy socks.

He reached the row where she crouched at the same time the first two police units entered the parking area. He waved and she spotted him. Then he motioned for her to come. He knew the police would fan out and check this lot, every row, every car, and that meant they required a new hiding place.

They'd be searching low, so they needed to go high. He scanned the lot for some means of escape. The young officer, the first responder, had remained posted at the alley. This gave him a view of much of the lot. The responding officers were blocking the two accesses to the road. But without a vehicle, the road didn't appeal.

Ryan clasped her hand and kept low, crouching as they jogged together back in the direction of the first responder. Ryan waited at the first row of vehicles to see if the young man would leave his post. The lure of the other officers' arrival being the bait.

Ryan lay down to watch the young officer's legs. He took a few steps toward them, speaking on his radio. Telling them that the woman had not left the lot. He walked forward, pausing before the bumpers of the cars parked closest to the access alley. That might be the farthest he went. Ryan took the chance. He squeezed her hand and pointed in the direction he intended them to go.

She nodded her understanding and he glanced back. The officer must've stepped between two vehicles, because Ryan could no longer see him.

If he turned his head, he'd spot them. If they made any sound they'd be caught. Ryan knew his chances against a young officer were good, but they dropped considerably against three officers. Add Haley to the mix and this was his best shot.

He darted out from cover, keeping low and gripping Haley's hand as if she were his mission. He didn't understand it. Couldn't think about it right now. He just had to get them to the row of four dumpsters.

When they cleared the closest one and reached the brick wall at the rear of the building, he paused, listening. The sirens stopped but red lights still reflected off the metal screen door just to their left.

Haley's breathing was fast and frantic. He glanced at her and saw her color was bad, too pale, and her irises too large and black. From the position behind the dumpsters, Ryan contemplated his next move. If they were spotted his chances of getting them both clear were poor. If they reached the rooftops, they'd be stranded for hours at least.

Ryan looked out from between the dumpsters. Then he crept forward to watch the search in progress. The officers crouched, focusing on a methodical search of each row of vehicles.

Now or never.

He climbed to the dumpster lid and offered his hand. She accepted without hesitation and he dragged her soundlessly up. From there it was an easy hop to the fire escape. He was glad for the approach of a new police unit. Still out of sight, its siren blared, covering the sound of their feet as they scaled the metal stairs. At each landing, he glanced into the apartments. Some were covered with curtains but others showed glimpses of a living room. The third landing had a potted plant left out and strategically placed to catch the drips of the window AC unit. It was the sort of thing one did when they planned to be away.

They reached the top of the fire escape. He paused to glance down. The police, six officers now, continued their search pattern. Any one of the men below could spot them if they were to look up.

But people rarely did.

"We have to get all the way to the roof," he said.

Haley glanced from him to the roof that lay twelve feet above where they now stood.

"How?"

"Escape rail and then I'll boost you up."

"Are you crazy?"

"So they tell me."

"What about you?"

"I'll climb."

Haley looked back at the brick wall. She backed up into him and then spun in his arms.

"I can't."

He gripped her shoulders and growled in her ear. "You can."

She dropped to her knees on the escape. Below them the sirens ceased. Curious folks had arrived to watch the hunt. Time was against them. Spectators would spot them eventually. He wished he had his poncho. He might cover her up so she looked like a grill or chair or garbage bin on the top escape. As it was he needed them off this metal staircase.

He scrambled up to the railing and reached. The roof lay another two feet beyond his extended arms, but in between lay the wooden sashing of the large window and above that the dental molding and lip of the flat roof.

Ryan bent his knees in preparation to jump and something clamped about his leg. He glanced down to find Haley, her face white, her hair sticking out in all directions.

Ryan offered a hand and she climbed up beside him. He waited until she braced against the building and then he jumped, easily reaching the roof's edge. The next part was more difficult. He had only his fingers over the edge. He managed a straight pull up and then lift until his arms were extended and his hips pressed to the metal flashing. He threw his leg up and scrambled onto the roof.

There he removed his flannel shirt and tied a loop in one sleeve and a knot in the other. Then he lay on his belly, pushed the shirt over the edge toward Haley, retaining a tight hold of the knot.

From his position, he saw that the officers were gathering beside one of the units. They would have a fine look at him, with his plaid flannel shirt, waving like a flag of surrender.

He returned his attention to Haley staring up at him, trembling as she clung to the building. He pantomimed slipping the loop of his sleeve over her wrist. She followed his silent instructions and clasped the other hand around the first. He hauled her up, gratified that she folded at the waist and used her legs to help push herself along. Finally, he grasped her wrist and dragged her the rest of the way onto the roof.

She rolled to her back on the gravel-and-tar covering, panting, one arm over her eyes.

"Bouldering," she said at last.

"What?"

"One of the things at adventure camp that I swore I

would never do. It's scrambling up rocks, climbing with no equipment except your helmet, some tiny shoes and the chalk on your fingers."

"Well, you did it without the chalk," he said, squatting beside her, untying the knots in his shirt and slipping it back on.

She lifted her arm from her pretty blue eyes. Her pupils had constricted against the sunlight and her eyes seemed to reflect the blue sky above.

"What now?" she asked.

"We stay put. They'll be searching for you, gradually extending their perimeter. The men chasing me will know soon that you were spotted. They'll redirect to this area."

She pushed to her seat. "Then shouldn't we leave?"

He shook his head. "There are two ways to elude capture. One is to run. The other is to hide."

"Hide? Here?" she squeaked.

"Good vantage point. Highest structure in town so no one can spot us except by helicopter. So we wait for dark."

He glanced up, knowing that eight or more hours on this roof in the summer heat would be rough. At least they had a breeze off the lake.

"Why did you leave the truck?" he asked, not looking at her as he studied their surroundings and made a plan. He assumed she saw now how dangerous that decision had been. The net was now tightening about them.

"I told you I had to call my dad. I needed to hear his voice."

"You could have been killed."

She didn't answer. Haley sniffed. A glance confirmed his suspicions. She was crying. She used a hand to swipe at the tears, brushing them away and leaving dirt and roofing tar streaked across her cheek.

He couldn't stop himself from pulling her into his arms. He made all the sounds that his mom used to make when he was crying. Her shoulders shook as she choked on sobs.

"You came back for me," she said at last.

He stroked her hair, using his fingers to comb out the tangles.

"Why did you do that?" she asked, lifting her face up to look at him.

The earnest expression and the trembling lower lip were his undoing.

"You needed help."

"But you said that nothing can interfere."

He wrapped his arms about her and rested his chin on the top of her head. She did interfere. Before meeting Haley he was more than ready to take risks, calculated risks to achieve his mission. Now he only wanted to see her safe.

When had that happened? When had his plans included seeing her through this? He thought it was the instant he saw her running for her life and knew that it was his fault.

"You remember when you asked me why I do this and I said it was for my country?"

"Yes."

"That wasn't the complete truth."

Chapter Fourteen

Haley blinked at him.

He'd told her he'd joined the Agency because he wanted to protect this country, or something of the like. It was how he always answered, a knee-jerk response as if she'd asked a police officer why he'd joined the force and was told, *To protect and serve.*

But there were as many reasons to join a law enforcement agency as there were to join an organization whose main purpose was to protect the sovereignty of the United States of America. He did want to serve his country, but if that was an answer, it was not the complete answer.

"Then what was the reason you became an agent?" she asked.

"Did I tell you anything about my dad?"

"You said he was older when you were born and that he died of liver cancer when you were twelve."

Thinking of his parents always made him sad. "He also worked a job he hated, paid his bills on time and did exactly what was expected of him at work, at home, in life. But he had all these plans, you know? My dad had plans for retirement. Plans for a big anniversary trip with my mom. Plans to fix the kitchen up and plans to buy a little fishing cabin in the Catskills. He never did any of them."

"Maybe they were just dreams or a way for him to get through what was ahead of him," she said. "An incentive to get up every morning."

"Trouble was, he moved from one thing to the next until he was diagnosed with the cancer." Ryan slapped his hand on the roof. "Even then he wouldn't take my mom to Quebec City like she wanted or himself on that fishing trip while he was still able. He was saving, not for his dreams anymore but to take care of my mom after he was gone. He never went anywhere or did anything that he said he wanted to do. And then he was gone. He only ever took his one-week vacation in Maine every year."

"Seashore?"

"Camping. It's cheaper. We stayed on public lands in a canvas tent that was older than he was. We'd paddle around in a battered old aluminum canoe. He'd fish and I'd swat mosquitoes."

"Did you like it?" she asked.

"He liked it there and that was plenty for me. Heading out he always looked so happy. But coming back he looked like someone had drained all the air out of him."

Ryan didn't know when he had wrapped his arms around his knees or when she had curled up beside him to rub his back.

She made a humming sound in her throat.

"My father worked all his life for the city of Albany. He drove a plow in Albany in the winter and supervised road repair the rest of the year. Do you have any idea how many potholes come up after the frost heave? He used to tease that there were only two seasons, winter and road construction. Anyway, he never took my mom on that trip to Quebec City that she wanted. Never took me on that fishing trip in Alaska that he wanted. He just drove that plow in circles until he was too sick to drive. Then they put him on disability, then he died. No pension because he never put in the paperwork to retire. Kept thinking he'd get back to work. Never did."

"So you take risks because he never did?" she asked.

That was part of it, he thought.

"Taking risks isn't as dangerous as reaching the end of your life and realizing you never lived."

"See, *my* plan is to reach the end of my life as far from today as possible."

He laughed. "Worse things than dying."

"If you say so. But did you ever consider that it wasn't your dad's death that was meaningful? It was his life."

"Working a job he hated?"

"Taking care of his family. Loving your mother. Raising a boy who made him proud."

Ryan flushed. "I'd rather die on a mission than in a hospital bed."

"Those aren't the only two options. And I'm sure he wouldn't want this for you. Though I know that what you are doing would make him proud."

"How could you know that?"

"Because I know his son and because I'm proud of you."

He glanced away, tugging at the collar of his shirt.

"And your father's life was full of meaning and of joys. Loving is important. More important than how you die."

He narrowed his eyes on her. She was dangerously close to judging him and finding him lacking. He was here to protect the lives of men and women he'd never meet. Maybe thousands of them. He shouldn't have come back for her. He should leave her at the first chance. His stomach clenched. How would he let her go?

"You telling me that loving a woman is more important than delivering the intelligence that could stop our enemies from domestic terrorism?"

"I think what you are doing is brave and admirable. But living a life, a full life that is rich with birthdays and one-week vacations and teaching your boy to ride a bike, it's just as admirable."

Ryan rubbed his neck. "How did you know he taught me to ride a bike?"

She smiled. "Just what fathers do, if you're lucky. Seems you were."

It was then he recalled that she still had both her parents, but her family had broken apart over a loss.

"How is your father?" he asked.

"He's all right."

"Anything unusual happening?"

"He didn't mention anything."

Ryan made a note to try to get word to his contacts and get her father and mother some protection. The trouble was that his communications could be compromised. Somehow their enemies had known where to find him and his courier.

Haley wasn't an operative, but her parents would make excellent pawns. His pursuers would by now know that she had been located. Would they guess that he had not abandoned her as expected?

"Why are the police after me?" she asked.

"Might be your accident and that you abandoned the scene. Could be the men posing as DEA put in a fake BOLO for you."

"BOLO?" she asked.

"Be On The Lookout. It's almost like an arrest warrant. I need to get us out of Lake George Village before our company shows up." He glanced toward the roof's edge. "Wait here."

She sat up straight, eyes going wide, but did as he asked. He moved to the edge, dropping to give the least visible target possible. A quick glance showed all the police officers still in the lot. But there were also two black vans with men dressed in plain clothes and carrying weapons on their hips.

He returned to her, weighing the risks of holding this position against moving higher on the roof.

He glanced around, realizing that this was the museum building, the one he had stood beside when retrieving Takashi's note. In the center of the roof lay three air-conditioning handlers with rusty housings and water puddling beneath the units. *Water,* he thought, ticking off one of the four things most needed for survival. The others were food and fire, not necessary here, and shelter. The center of the roof slanted upward from all four sides. Atop the highest point sat a rudely constructed turret, to add a certain character to the exterior of the building and made it look more gothic, he supposed. He turned his head sideways.

"What?" she asked.

"Looks more like something from a Zorro movie than Frankenstein. More hacienda than castle. But it will give us cover from the sun." *Two out of three*, he thought.

"First, I'm not climbing up that inclined roof. Second, anyone can see us once we leave this part."

"We'll wait here until the police move off. Then I'll pick up some supplies."

"Where from?"

"There was a window open down the fire escape and plants left out on the landing." She was right that they might be spotted from the street while climbing up the incline to the structure at the peak. But Haley's skin was already pink and he knew she'd burn to a crisp if they had to spend the entire day with no cover.

Indecision weighed on him. If not for her, he'd remain here. Her needs were interfering with his decision-making. Adding risk.

The sound of a helicopter made the decision easier. The minute he could see it, those aboard could see him.

"Up!" he shouted. "Move."

He clasped her hand and tugged her toward the inclined roof, scrambling along on the street side, opposite the police presence. He gripped her tight as she used her feet and free hand to propel herself to the turret.

Once on the top, he lifted her into the structure that he now thought might have been intended to resemble a bell tower. He rolled in behind her. His landing shook the structure.

Haley huddled against one of the sides of the six-square-foot box that was shingled on the outside with large scalloped cutouts to mimic the arched openings of the second-floor balcony below and a peaked roof above.

He crouched beside her as the helicopter moved closer, hovering over the lot. He moved them to the opposite wall. If he couldn't see them, they couldn't see him or Haley.

"Is that them?" she asked.

He nodded and wrapped an arm around her. She huddled against him as the chopper hovered for a long while. Then it began to circle their position.

"How can they expect to spot us amid all the tourists?"

"It's just one prong of the search."

It was well into the afternoon before the helicopter finally moved off. He assumed the police had left as well, but there was no reason for them to move until dark.

Haley's face was flushed and she was sweating in the heat. She needed water, but that would have to wait.

"Did you find what you were looking for?" she asked.

He patted the zipped pocket. "Yes. Takashi used the drop. But it's not the flash drive." He unzipped the pocket and removed the envelope. Then he slit open the seal with his index finger.

Inside was a single page, which read:

Travel Around the World
to Mexico's man-made shade.

Ryan turned over the page.

He cursed under his breath. This wasn't some scavenger hunt.

"Why would he leave something so cryptic?" he asked.

She looked up at him and he handed over the note. "Perhaps he wanted to be sure his pursuers couldn't find the package, even if they found this."

"Well, I can't find it, either."

"Didn't you say that you and your parents vacationed here?"

"No, but you have. Right?" he asked.

"Many times."

"Well, he didn't have time to get to Mexico. So what do you think this means?" he asked and handed her the page.

"There's a Mexico, New York," she offered.

Ryan shook his head as he dismissed the idea. "Too broad and too far away. This has to point to a specific place. Somewhere nearby. He planted the package and then we met. He told me where to find this note. I thought it would be the intel. During our meeting, we were spotted and forced to flee."

"And they got him?"

"According to those women. It might be a lie. I hope it's a lie." He accepted the note back and checked the back and held it up to see if there might be something he had missed. "Well, Mexico, huh? Man-made shade. Like a house or a veranda?"

He thought about the cryptic note but could make nothing of it.

Haley yawned. "Why not just tell you where to find it? If you can't figure it out, we can't recover the data. And if you could figure it out, couldn't your pursuers?"

He shook his head. "I just have to..."

Haley nestled against him and closed her eyes. The exhaustion of the day had caught her. He'd cornered them in this hiding spot. For better or worse, they could not move now, so he followed her example, stowing away the clue and closing his eyes.

Rest when you can, move when you must.

When he opened his eyes, he had a crick in his neck and was stretched out on his back with his neck and knees bent at an odd angle. Haley lay tucked in the crook of his arm as if she belonged there. Maybe she did.

She'd disobeyed an order and she'd given away their position. He should be furious with her. Instead he felt a warm glow just looking at her sleeping features.

He lifted a strand of hair that fell across his chest and rubbed it between his finger and thumb. He'd spent more time with Haley than he had any woman in years. He'd never wanted to get attached before. Now he discovered that he already was.

She sighed and made a sound like purring in the

back of her throat. Then she stretched her legs, which thumped against the confines of their hideaway. The purr became a groan as one hand moved to her neck. She blinked her eyes open and looked at him.

"Oh, man, what a neck ache."

"Hmm," he said, both relieved and bereft when she pushed herself to a seated position.

"What time is it?" she asked, glancing about.

The streetlights below them cast enough light to prevent him from seeing the stars.

"I'm not sure. Time to move."

He stood and looked out at the lake, glimmering brighter than anything else around them.

She stood beside him. "I wanted to ask you, how did those men find you?"

He had spent a good deal of time puzzling over that.

"I'm not sure. As soon as I made contact, the drop, it all went sideways. I don't know if the breach was on our end or Takashi's. I hope it's his end. I prefer that to the alternative."

"Which is?"

"My supervisor is dirty."

He stepped out onto the roof and turned to her. She accepted his hand but climbed out without any other assistance. Together they crept back down to the flat section of roof and then to the fire escape.

"How do we even do this?" she asked.

Haley had not spent the last eight years on obstacle courses and training in various scenarios. He walked her through it.

"You lie flat. Slide one leg over, then the other. Hang from the ledge and drop onto the fire escape."

"Is that all?" She pressed a hand to her hip.

"That's all."

"I can't do that."

He smiled at her. "Yes, you can."

She knew she had no choice. It was the only option. Haley lay on the roof as he instructed. She even slid a leg over on her own. He gripped her wrists as she slipped off the safety of the roof and then he lowered her to within a foot of the landing.

"Bend your knees to absorb your landing. Ready?"

She stared up at him with wide, frightened eyes and then nodded. He let go.

Haley landed in a crouch like a superhero. He smiled. Whether she believed it or not, she was a natural. He dropped beside her a moment later. Before them was the dark window and beside him was the waterlogged plant.

"Nobody home," he said. He reached for the window to the left of the escape. It held a flimsy accordion plastic that filled the gap between the partial window frame and the room AC unit set in the opening.

"What are you doing?"

"Getting us some supplies." With the plastic retracted, it was an easy matter to lift the window. He set the AC on the landing of the fire escape and stepped inside. Haley followed.

The combo living and dining room was dark and empty. The lights from the parking lot beyond supplied ample illumination for him to see the neat stack of mail on the circular table. Letters in one pile, magazines in another and catalogs in still another. Someone, a neighbor perhaps, was keeping an eye on things, picking up the mail.

That meant he had time.

He lifted the AC back into the apartment, shut and locked the window. His initial recon showed that this couple, like many, had opted to remove their landlines. In other words, he found no phone with which to check in. He booted up their computer and was faced with a password request. Checking under the keyboard, mouse pad and corkboard yielded nothing. He flipped off the computer.

His next stop was the kitchen sink, where he drank from the spigot. Then he encouraged Haley to do the same, but she retrieved a glass from the dish rack instead. Once she'd had her fill, he shut off the stream.

"Go in the bedroom and see if you can find a bag, knapsack or large purse. Also a change of clothing."

"Who lives here?" she asked.

He lifted a bit of mail and read. "Mr. and Mrs. Todd Weller." Then he returned the mail to the pile and glanced up at her. "Let's hope Todd is a large and Mrs. Todd is a small."

She headed through the doorway and then appeared a moment later.

"May I use the bathroom?" she whispered.

"Yes. Use whatever you want but leave everything exactly as it is."

She disappeared and he rummaged in the drawers collecting cordage, a lighter. He heard the toilet flush and the water run. He left his rummaging to search the bedroom. He lay out clothing on the bed for each of them, then she emerged to stand beside him, looking down at the selections.

"Took things from the bottom of each drawer. With luck they won't even miss them."

He excused himself to use the bathroom and found an old claw-foot tub anchoring the room. He finished and took a moment to wash his face, surprised at the amount of grit on his skin. When he returned to her it was to find her staring at the bed with arms folded.

"I hate to get into clean clothing when I'm this filthy," she said.

He wouldn't usually indulge himself but Haley surely deserved to bathe. He'd keep watch.

"Okay, just a quick shower."

She clapped her hands and spun. Then she disappeared into the bathroom. He stuffed the clothing into his bag on the chance they'd have to make a fast exit. Then he returned to the living room and bolted the door.

If the neighbor looking after things made an appearance, he or she would not be able to get in.

Premises secure, he returned to the bedroom, where he heard the sound of water.

He opened the door. She showered in the darkness. Filtered blue light crept in from the window behind the bathtub, making the outline of her form visible.

"Haley? Do you have a towel?"

"No. Isn't there one on the holder?"

"Nope. I'll find something." It didn't take long to discover the linen closet. He collected two towels and retraced his steps. When he returned he told her that the towels were on the sink.

"Are you going to shower?"

He hadn't planned to but with Haley naked in the cascading water, he thought the idea too tempting to resist.

"Sure. Let me know when you're done."

"Just let me get the soap from my eyes." A moment later the water flicked off and her hand emerged. "Towel?"

He extended it to her. The shower curtain billowed as she dried and then emerged with the towel wrapped around herself and rolled to remain in place—unless he gave a sharp tug.

His fingers itched as he resisted the impulse.

"That felt wonderful!" She grinned. "Your turn. Go on."

He tugged off his shirt and let it fall in the pile of her clothing. She stepped back, the smile replaced with a wide-eyed stare.

"Nothing you haven't seen," he said.

He unfastened the cargo pants and she spun around, presenting him with her back. He took a moment to notice that her hair curled in ringlets and dripped into the absorbent towel. Water droplets rolled down her long bare legs.

Ryan stepped out of his pants and briefs, glad that she didn't see him, dirty, aroused and hungry as a wolf to taste that sweet damp flesh. He stepped into the tub and dragged the curtain around him.

A moment later he was under a cascade of warm water. The abrasions stung. He washed quickly but not so quickly that the water did not transition from warm to cold. Just what he needed, he thought.

He flicked off the water and the towel appeared before him on Haley's extended arm.

"Thanks."

He dried off and told himself he was not getting lucky. For one thing, Haley was not that sort of woman. For another, he had a rule about sleeping with women who he might see again. He didn't do it because once you had sex, everything changed. Women became more demanding.

But he was tempted.

He wrapped the towel around his waist and dragged the curtain away.

She was using a finger to brush her teeth and offered him the tube. Then she rinsed her mouth and gargled. The sound made him smile, it was so guileless and normal. She rummaged in the medicine cabinet and found deodorant spray. She bounced with delight and then applied a liberal amount.

Haley borrowed a comb and face cream and lotion, returning everything exactly where she had found it. The sight of her rubbing the lavender-scented cream down her long legs caused a sharp pang of desire.

He didn't sleep with women he liked. It was another rule to keep him from getting too attached. And he liked Haley enough to risk his mission for her. It was baffling.

"Want some?" she asked.

He shook his head.

"Come on, I'll rub it into your back." She stepped

behind him. "Should feel good on those healing scabs. Keep them from breaking open."

Before he could stop her, her gentle hands were massaging the lotion into his skin. She kneaded his sore muscles and stroked down the center of his back. He gripped the sink and just kept himself from groaning in pleasure.

"Feel good?" she asked, the mirth evident in her voice.

"So good."

She stepped around him and pressed the lotion bottle into his chest. "You can reach the rest."

He gripped the lotion when he wanted to grip her.

She strode from the bathroom on bare feet. By the time he had collected himself enough to follow, Haley had dropped her towel and was sliding into a man's T-shirt that gaped at the neck. He should have waited.

"That one was for me."

He caught sight of the tempting curve of her backside and the perfect symmetry of her back before the top fell into place, reaching mid-thigh.

"We need to find you something that fits."

He knew why that didn't. The photo on the bureau showed a fortyish couple who were both running toward XXL.

She turned toward him and smiled, unaware of the hurricane of desire swirling inside him.

"This is good for now," she said. "I'm going to get us something to eat and then I'll try to find something smaller."

She was going to walk around in nothing but a T-shirt?

His body ached at the thought of what lay beneath that thin sheath of cotton.

"No lights," he said.

He watched her go, wondering what she would do if he took her in his arms and kissed her like he wanted. Instead he stripped off the towel and used it on his hair. Then he dressed for travel in a black T-shirt and wool crew neck sweater. The pants were a problem, as each pair he tried on was miles too big. He settled for clean socks and his dirty cargo pants. They had the capability to carry small items and they fit.

When he reached the kitchen it was to the rhythmic sound of Haley beating eggs.

"Not much in the fridge. They must have cleaned it out before leaving. But I found bread, cheese and eggs. So, omelet and toast, all right?"

"Perfect." Ryan continued loading gear into the bag he'd commandeered. He was ready to travel as she finished cooking, slipped a huge omelet onto a plate and then set it on the table.

"You eat," she said and turned back to the stove.

The food all but disappeared and he was just finishing his toast when she sat with a smaller portion. Haley did not take any extra time in finishing off her meal. When she sat back, they shared a smile.

"I feel almost human again. What a luxury."

"You've been very brave through all this," he said.

"Brave?" she laughed. "That's ridiculous."

"It isn't. You've kept up, handled all unanticipated obstacles well. I'd be happy to work with you as an agent."

She gaped at him. "If my dad could only hear you say that."

Haley stood to clear the table and he followed her to the sink. She washed and he dried. Then they put the items away exactly as they had been, minus the bread, butter, eggs and cheese.

"Think they'll notice?" she asked.

"Not immediately. They'll suspect the person they gave access to."

"And the clothing?"

"Hard to notice what is missing. Much easier to spot something that doesn't belong."

She turned off the tap and replaced the sponge on the drying rack. "What now?"

HE WAS SMILING down at her and she noted a definite change in the air. It felt charged with energy, some invisible zip that danced between them.

"Ryan?" she said, tentative now.

He turned and placed his hands on her hips. She stepped forward, resting a damp hand on his shoulder. He smelled of soap and aftershave. She admired the clean planes of his cheeks and the strong line of his jaw.

"You shaved," she said and could not resist stroking the smooth skin.

He hummed and pressed his cheek against her palm as his eyes fluttered closed for a moment. Then he straightened, looking down at her.

"I want to thank you," he said. "If you hadn't stopped for me, I'd be dead and the mission a failure. If you hadn't distracted that young state police officer, I would have had to disarm him and our escape would have been in jeopardy. I was serious when I said you are a brave woman. The one you described, the one who can't handle risk, I haven't seen her."

She smiled at the compliment. Somehow she felt more herself with Ryan than she did alone in her apartment in Brooklyn. It was almost as if she had been sleeping all those years.

"I'm glad I stopped. Glad to have met you, Ryan."

His smile remained but there was some new spark in his eyes. He angled his head, as if preparing to kiss her, but hesitated.

"Are you going to kiss me?" she asked.

"I shouldn't."

So she kissed him.

She stepped in and gave him a taste of the heat she now felt tingling through her bloodstream. He hesitated, held back, just as he had in the field. She pressed tight to him and raked her fingers through his hair. She felt the moment of surrender when he dove full force into their kiss. Haley gasped as he took control of her, cradling her head as he bent her over his arm. Her tongue darted into his mouth, gliding against his as she purred deep in the back of her throat. His kisses trailed over her neck and to the shell of her ear.

He lifted her to the counter and she wrapped her legs around him. She'd had an IUD for years, part of her careful, cautious lifestyle and a model way to be in control of even her body's cycles.

She felt the hard evidence of his desire pressed against her needy flesh.

"You sure about this?" he whispered against her neck.

"So sure."

He lifted her from the counter and swept down the hall to the bathroom, where he let her slide down his body as he retrieved something from the medicine cabinet. A black box of condoms. Ribbed, according to the label.

He let her select a square packet and then threw her over his shoulder and carried her to the bed.

Haley had had chances to be with a man. She'd taken a few, always choosing wisely and carefully. But tonight, she would not be wise or careful. She knew full well the uncertainty that lay beyond that door and she was not going to waste a moment of this precious time together with doubts or worry. She wanted him and, for once, she was taking what she wanted without calculating the risk and reward, without consideration or second-guessing.

As she fell back on the bed, she stretched her arms wide in welcome to the man who had reminded her that life was for the living.

Chapter Fifteen

Ryan lay replete on the sheets of someone else's bed, knowing they should be moving locations but unable to muster the energy to do more than drag Haley's lush body against his. The predawn gloom filtered soft light though the closed window curtains and over Haley naked in his arms.

He thought back to the kisses they'd shared and how he had moved inside her silken, yielding body. Haley's movements offered just the right resistance and friction, making that first time absolutely the most mind-blowing experience of his life. Too perfect. Her cries of pleasure had triggered his own. Simultaneously, they had found their release.

It had happened naturally, a response to their unity. In the past, every time he'd managed such a feat it had been a measure of his control, restraint and consummate timing.

He'd tried to please Haley, but in the center of their time together, he'd forgotten his moves and his timing and his consummate control and just savored the feel of her.

He cared about her. That was both the reason and the trouble. Nothing good would come of this.

He sat up in the darkness, suddenly cold, his heart hammering and his body bathed in sweat. What was happening to him? Was he sick?

"Ryan?" Her voice was sleepy, as if she had dragged her words from a long way away. "What's wrong?"

"I don't know."

She pulled herself up and moved behind him. He swung his legs over the edge of the bed and she slipped her hands around his chest, pressing her bare body to his back.

He shuddered at the pleasure of her warmth.

"You're trembling," she said, her voice now edged with concern. She lifted her head. "Did you hear something?"

As if that would make him shake.

"No. Go back to sleep." He hadn't meant for his voice to sound so cross.

She pulled away.

"Why are you sweating? Bad dream?"

Haley knelt beside him now, her face cast in shadows as she stared at him, not giving up.

"It was a bad idea."

"What, sleeping together?"

"Yes."

"Why?"

"Because you're different than most women in my world. You're not the sort to just…" He waved a hand at the rumpled coverlet. "I know you well enough to understand that you set a high value on relationships."

"I don't see how that is a problem."

His expression turned melancholy. "When I finish this, if I finish this, you won't see me again."

She frowned. "Is that true?"

He nodded.

"Why?"

"Relationships, they're a liability. A weapon that can be used against me."

She lifted her brows and then shook her head.

"Maybe. But that's not why."

His mouth was too dry to speak. What was this? He felt like he might be having a heart attack.

Haley aimed a finger at him. "This isn't about me or my feelings. This isn't about the danger a relationship will cause me. It is about the danger it poses to you. You don't like to get close to people for the same reason I don't like taking chances." She slipped off the bed and into the discarded T-shirt to stand before him in the near dark. "I've been trying to see that nothing happens to me because my mother told me point-blank that she'd never survive my loss. So I did everything I could to limit risks, but I never realized that in seeing to not dying, I stopped living. And I got what I wanted. Absolutely nothing has happened to me." She lifted a finger and aimed it at him. "You have room in your world and your heart, Ryan. You just aren't as brave as you pretend to be."

He shook his head. "That doesn't make any sense."

"No? You're so interested in making sure that your death matters, you forgot that you're alive. Living people have relationships."

Ryan pushed off the bed and stalked away, retrieving his boxers at the foot of the bed and dragging them on.

"That's stupid."

"Then tell me the last relationship you had that lasted more than a few hours?"

He stopped dead and turned to her.

How did she know that?

"Meanwhile every time I get close to someone or start to have a really good time, I feel this stab of guilt." Her voice cracked and she choked out the rest. "I still miss her. I feel so guilty being here."

"No reason to feel guilty for not dying."

"Not over surviving. Over living." She crumpled on the bed. "For laughing and loving, while my sister—"

"It's not your fault."

"And it's not your fault that your dad died so early. I didn't know him, but I do know he would not want this for you."

"I'm serving my country."

"You are taking on the most dangerous missions possible. Tempting fate. You know the ironic part? Even if you do succeed and your death saves thousands of lives, no one will know about it. No one will grieve your passing because you kept everyone at arm's length. And the world won't even know your name."

That was all true but hearing her say it out loud felt like a blade slicing across his bare stomach. He pressed a palm to his abdomen and sank down beside her, the mattress sagging.

"There are worse things," he said. "Like being so careful you miss all the joy."

She looked away and he knew he'd scored a hit. Somehow it didn't make him feel any better.

"I just want to find somewhere safe," she whispered.

"There's nowhere safe. You just have to go on in spite of that."

She lifted her chin and stared up at him, casting a sad smile. "I'm not brave enough to do that."

Was that why she hadn't found a man, married and had a few children? All because her sister's death stopped her from enjoying anything?

"What about children?" he asked.

"What about them?"

"Do you want them?"

She rolled her eyes. "They're a mess."

The answer seemed glib.

"Haley, really?"

She dropped her affectations and lowered her gaze "It scares me. Having a child seems too dangerous."

"Giving birth, you mean?"

"No. I mean all the terrible things that can go wrong before you give birth and afterwards. Having them is the easy part. Then there's raising them. Worrying about them. Teaching them to take risks, but not too many risks or the wrong kind. Protecting them and knowing you can never fully protect them. The world is a wide field of land mines of possible catastrophes."

He looped an arm around her waist and drew her in. She settled her head against his shoulder.

"Aren't we a pair?"

He tightened his hold, drawing her into a firm embrace. This is what he wanted—to hold her. Her body was as warm as a campfire on a cold night.

"So is that all that is between us? One night? One mistake?" she asked.

"I don't know. Time will tell, I suppose." He was all mixed up inside. The insistent tug of attraction still pulled. Her body tingled as his fingers drew rhythmic circles on her back. Their time together in this little sanctuary was nearly over. They'd already stayed too long. "We need to move on."

"Yes, of course. Where will we go?"

"They'll have a roadblock barring access to the Northway. Our photos will have been circulated among law enforcement."

"Maybe we should just stay here for a while."

He knew it was tempting but this place was too close to their near-capture and it did not help him solve the riddle Takashi had left him.

"They'll expect us to take a car. So we take a boat."

"A motorboat?"

"No, sheriff will be checking those, too, I'm afraid. We're taking a small craft."

She stiffened. "How small?"

He didn't answer.

"Not a kayak," she whispered.

"That's what I was thinking. Why?"

She groaned. "It's one of the adventure camp activities. One that I put a line through."

He chuckled. "What else did you cross off?"

"Cliff jumping and zip line." She dipped her chin. "Everything. I crossed them all off."

"Then why did you agree to go?" he asked.

"Nonrefundable gift."

"That's not why."

"My dad wanted me to get out there." She made a face and then said, "He said that I wasn't the one who had died."

Ryan's mouth quirked. "I agree with his motives, but tossing you off a cliff, it's extreme."

"He did it out of love."

Ryan nodded. "I'll try to keep us off cliffs." He drew her to her feet. "Find something you can wear. Nothing too bright or memorable."

"The gray man," she said.

"How do you know about that?"

"I read it in a magazine article in my dentist's office. The gray man is not actually gray, just blends into the crowd. Unremarkable."

"Exactly. And we're out for a kayak ride on the lake."

"Got it."

Ryan disappeared into the bathroom. The door shut behind him. Haley looked in the bureau for something more her size and replaced the things he'd laid out for her in the bottom drawer.

She came up with a white tankini and a V-neck T-shirt in a dull orange-brown. A windbreaker in forest green that she tied around her hips and a pair of beige capri pants with a canvas belt that kept them up.

Ryan emerged from the bathroom and nodded his approval before she stepped past him to use the facilities, wash her face and comb her hair. Since she usually wore it down, she opted for a ponytail.

She folded the towels and stepped out of the bedroom to find the coverlet again neatly draped over the queen-size bed. She returned the towels to the linen closet.

Ryan stood in the kitchen beside the microwave. The time on the clock flipped from 5:59 to 6:00 a.m. He was in familiar cargo pants. The dark T-shirt fit well. The backpack looped over one shoulder and he wore a ball cap on his head and offered her a similar one. She adjusted the size and slipped it on, pulling her ponytail through the hole in the back.

"Ready?" he asked, one hand on the door.

"That way?" she said, surprised they would not go out the fire escape.

"Low profile. We head out and walk to the docks. Find a kayak and go."

"Where?"

"Out of the village for now, until I figure out that clue Takashi left me."

Haley drew a breath and held it. When she nodded, he opened the door. She released her breath with a prayer that they would make it safely away.

The stairway let them out into an alley beside the building. The sky was lightening, a sign of the approaching sunrise. They reached the street and Ryan paused.

Haley watched a woman sifting through a large recycle bin, extracting the cans. Ryan nodded and they headed down the street at a pace she found far too slow. Her heart raced as her feet sauntered. They passed the woman, who glanced up at them and then returned to her work.

A single car approached, the headlights blinding. Ryan slowed.

"Hey! Stop right there!"

Haley jumped at the male voice shouting. A police officer stepped from his unit, standing in the space between the open door and his vehicle. For just a moment she thought it was the same officer as the day before. He started toward them.

Ryan gripped her trembling hand, staying her just as she turned to run.

Chapter Sixteen

Ryan hauled her to a stop as the police officer stepped past them.

"That's village property," said the officer to the woman scavenging cans.

Haley did not hear her words but the tone was antagonistic. Ryan set them in motion as Haley stumbled along. Her ears were ringing as if she'd suffered a head injury.

She glanced back to see the officer had collected the woman's booty and was waving her off. Inadvertently, the woman had provided them with a diversion. Ryan picked up their pace as they left the main drag and headed toward the lakeshore.

They were not the first to arrive. Several sailboats were already out on the water and the slips that held the fishing charters were empty.

The kayak rental stand was shut up, the kayaks stacked on racks and chained together. Also there were no paddles or life vests in sight.

The wind off the lake was chilly and Haley took a moment to slip into her new stolen windbreaker.

Ryan headed them toward the marina docks.

"Kayaks are that way," she whispered.

He ignored her and led them to the metal dock, which clanged with their footsteps as they moved along. He waved at a boater in his sailboat, fiddling with a coiled rope.

"Beautiful day," called the man.

"Just lovely," Haley said and continued on, to where, she was not sure. He stopped at the eight-foot-tall metal gate upon which hung a sign that read Private Dock. The wire-mesh-and-aluminum fencing jutted out on each side of the dock to prevent people like them from continuing on.

She glanced through the metal bars at the object of his desire, a huge boat, a ship perhaps, that held a Jet Ski on the back and four kayaks anchored to the top platform.

He tried the handle to the door and found it locked.

"Wait," he said.

She was about to object but he climbed up the door, doing a rolling thing over the top to land on the deck in a crouch. That move really belonged in a superhero movie. He grinned back at her from the opposite side.

The other side of the door was unlocked and so, a moment later, she stepped onto the private dock. He strolled before her like the captain of a vessel, passing the one with the Jet Ski in favor of one that she had not seen from the dock. Perhaps, she thought, that was the exact reason he picked it.

There was a gangplank to the dock, making boarding the vessel ridiculously easy.

"You're officially a pirate now," he told her.

She followed him to the front—the aft, she recalled—of the vessel. He did not try to break into the cabin or the captain's area up the ladder. Instead, he focused on untying a lime-green kayak. It was only when he began untying the royal blue one that she realized that kayaks, or perhaps just these particular kayaks, were one-person vessels.

"I can't row that," she said.

"Paddle," he said. "Up to you. But I'm sure your chances are better if you try."

"I won't be able to keep up with you."

"We are just going a few miles. Leisurely, like tourists. We'll find an empty cabin."

"On the week of July Fourth? You won't. I know this place. It is absolutely packed over this holiday. It's why we only made day trips until the fall. Prices go sky-high, tourists everywhere."

"Easier to blend in." He tipped the kayak onto his head and walked past her. She watched him go. If he thought she could lift the other one onto her head and walk, he'd lost his mind.

When he disappeared over the stern of the boat, she hurried after him, but once she reached the wide white plastic stairs at the stern, he was on his way back. He stepped past her and she glanced to the flat platform at the bottom of the stairs. It was like a connected dock for launching rafts and kayaks, apparently. She spun to watch his return, curious now as to how he got that sixteen-foot kayak soundlessly down a flight of stairs.

The answer was simpler than she expected. He simply lowered the boat to the top of the stairs and used the towline, which was connected to the loop at the front of the craft, to ease it down the stairs.

"What about paddles?" she asked.

In answer, he threw down two flotation vests and then descended the stairs, gripping the paddles in one hand.

He explained how to use the paddle, whose blades were offset in a way that made the paddling seem complicated, with a turn of the wrist and a pull and lift and…he clipped her into her vest, which was sunshine yellow.

He dropped the bag of gear into the blue kayak. Then he turned to her.

"Have a seat and I'll launch you."

"Like hell," she said.

"Really. You sit and I slide you in like I did on the stairs. Look."

He pointed to a ramp on the deck that she hadn't noticed.

"I'll tip over."

"Don't pull too hard when you paddle. Don't lean, either. The farther you lean the better the chance you'll tip."

These words inspired no confidence as he took her by the waist and propelled her from behind toward the green kayak. She was barely seated when the kayak moved.

"Wait," she said.

"Hands on the gunnels."

"What if I tip over?"

"Then you'll have to drag yourself back into your craft."

"I can't even do one pull-up," she said as the plastic scraped on the ramp and then she was floating, holding the paddle above her head as if in surrender.

Holy heck!

She still had the paddle over her head, trying not to move for fear of tipping, when she heard the scrape of the second kayak and turned.

Ryan had a look of pure exhilaration on his face as he swooshed into the water and began paddling to where she had drifted.

"What a rush," he said, grinning like a boy.

"Which? The stealing or the getaway?"

"We aren't away yet. Try your paddle. I can tow you, but it will draw notice."

Haley lowered her paddle across the kayak.

"Like this." He demonstrated, making the act of paddling look graceful and efficient.

For a moment she just enjoyed the pleasure of watching him. And as she gazed at him, his muscles bulging and relaxing in a rhythmic motion, she forgot she was bobbing along like a cork.

"You try."

She remembered, glanced back to the launch site and realizing she was drifting toward the dock. Her paddle tipped into the water and dragged along.

"Good," he encouraged, but his gaze was not on her but on the dock and the platform that was lifting up and rocking down with the motion of the water. "A little faster."

Haley had a perfect premonition of tipping, falling and then being sucked under the boat.

She set the paddle in the water and pulled. The kayak jettisoned forward. Haley gasped. Then she rocked the handle and tried the opposite side. She grinned. The kayak was reasonably stable and high enough in the water that paddling was easy, so much more easy than the canoe.

Ryan glided up beside her. He indicated his destination.

"Hug the shore, but not so tight that you could speak to anyone onshore. You set the pace."

She got to lead. The exhilaration and delight filled her up as she set off parallel to the shore and was nearly run down by a sailboat.

"Starboard, you idiot," called the woman at the back as she glided past under the power of only one small sail.

Haley smiled and waved. "You have a great boat."

The women flipped her the bird.

"Stay to the right of any vessel you see," said Ryan.

She needed that information about a minute earlier, she thought but said nothing as she concentrated on establishing a rhythm. They passed the swimming area in time to see the lifeguards taking their morning training swim en masse, around the swimming dock.

Ryan now traveled beside her.

"I used to swim to that," she said to him. "My sister and I would race." She smiled at the memory.

"We'd take a boat ride in the morning on the *Minne-Ha-Ha* and then swim in the afternoon. In the evening, we'd get hot dogs at the mini golf place and have ice cream when we reached the London Bridge."

She stopped paddling.

"What's wrong?" Ryan asked. His hand snaked out and grasped the edge of her seating compartment. "Haley?"

"I know what he meant."

"Who?"

"Takashi. Travel to Mexico. Man-made shade."

Chapter Seventeen

"You can retrieve the flash drive now. Complete your mission," said Haley.

Ryan gripped the side of her kayak. It was clear from her expression that she was excited and had reached some sort of epiphany.

"What are you talking about, Haley?"

"Man-made shade. It's a sombrero. Travel around the world. It's the mini golf course. There's one in Lake George. There are nine holes themed after attractions in the USA and the other nine are all international. One is Mexico! That's what he meant. Travel to Mexico. It's one of the holes on the mini golf course."

Ryan's eyes widened. She could be right. It made sense. After Ryan had provided Takashi with cover, he had escaped. They were in the vicinity of Lake George Village. He would have been looking for a place that was easy to find but also easily missed. Somewhere safe that he could tuck the flash drive where it would not be discovered by the wrong person. Clearly, he did not think the village of Lake George and their prearranged drop was safe.

"The mini golf course. Yes. I know where that is." Ryan glanced back to the public beach. Beyond was the bathhouse and just up the road was the miniature golf course and the hole called Mexico. He could be there and back in less than an hour. But he couldn't with Haley along.

He reviewed his directive. *Complete the mission. Deliver the intelligence.*

"Ryan?"

He hadn't realized that he had released her kayak and was drifting toward the swimming area. Then he noticed what she had been pointing at because two men on two Jet Skis were racing toward them.

"They're coming right at us," she said, clutching her paddle.

"Separate." *Force them to choose a target*, he thought.

They did. One man aimed a pistol at Haley. He heard the shot at the same time he saw her go over sideways in her kayak.

Their attacker kept coming, making right for him, pistol raised. But he didn't fire. His partner slowed to an idle and the shooter followed his lead. They wanted him, at least, alive.

Ryan's instinct was to dive in after Haley. He scanned the water but could see nothing but her upturned kayak. Her vest should bring her to the surface even if she was...

And then he saw the flash of pale legs kicking. She was under her kayak. He knew the plastic covering offered no protection from bullets but the approaching figure now had his attention fully on Ryan.

Was she injured?

The driver of the Jet Ski reached out his empty hand.

"Give it to me," he ordered.

"What?" Ryan gripped the paddle.

"We saw you collect the envelope."

Had they? Why didn't they move in then? And then Ryan remembered the police and DEA circling the neighborhood. They'd tried and failed to find him. Until now.

He glanced at Haley, seeing her strong legs rhythmically churning the water.

"I don't know what you're talking about."

"Give me the envelope," he repeated.

Ryan shook his head. "Listen, buddy—"

The man leading the inquiry turned to his partner.

"Kill the girl."

Ryan felt a cold flash of terror. He shivered with the panic that rocked him. He lifted a hand from the paddle.

"All right." Then he reached behind himself and unzipped the pocket in his bag. The shooter kept his pistol aimed at him now, off Haley, at least for the moment.

He watched Haley leave her hiding spot and swim away, toward the men who confronted them. She had discarded the yellow flotation vest and now glided like a seal under the first Jet Ski and disappeared from his line of sight. What was she doing?

Ryan retrieved the envelope and held it out. The man extended his hand and Ryan grabbed his wrist, planted his feet and pulled. They both went into the water, but his attacker fell into the kayak on his descent. By the time Ryan hit the water he had already shrugged out of his vest.

His combatant came up and shouted to his partner. "Kill him."

Ryan turned toward the shooter and swept both arms upward, which forced his body down. The last thing he saw werewas the silver streaming tails of the bullets penetrating the clear lake water above his head and beyond. At the surface, Haley stepped onto the back of the shooter's Jet Ski and launched herself at his extended arm.

Ryan forgot the envelope, directive and mission as he swam toward Haley. He emerged beside her as she hit the water. Ryan grabbed the shooter's waistband from the opposite side of the sled, planted his feet on the side of the Jet Ski and pushed off. They both went into the lake. Ryan jabbed him in the throat and both his opponent's hands came up as his airway went into spasms. He'd dropped the gun.

Ryan surfaced and glanced about. Haley was beside him, gripping the Jet Ski. A motor roared and the second man jetted away, sending a rooster tail spray over them all. Beside them the shooter surfaced, choking and coughing on lake water. Gasping as he tried and failed to breathe.

"Go get the drive!" Haley shouted.

"What about you?"

"Go, Ryan, or he'll get there first. He has the envelope!"

Ryan climbed onto the Jet Ski from the back and offered his hand. Haley scrambled up behind him. A moment later they were flying over the water. Ryan hunched and Haley clung. Behind them bobbed two abandoned kayaks, paddles, a vest and one would-be assassin.

They almost made it, too. Then Ryan saw the sheriff's boat drawing parallel to them. The young officer motioned for him to stop.

"Keep going," Haley said. "I'll slow them down."

"What?"

Before he could ask what she intended, Haley straightened and fell backward off the Jet Ski. The sheriff cut his engine. Ryan glanced back to see Haley flailing in the water, making a very good impression of a distressed swimmer.

They'd take her in, he was certain. How long until the men pursuing them came after Haley?

The Sheriff's boat drew alongside Haley, and Ryan sped away toward the agent carrying Takashi's message. These were new players. He was certain that he had not seen either of them before and he was unsure if they were with the agents impersonating DEA or perhaps ones from the Chinese government where Takashi had stolen the information.

Why did he feel this tugging urge to turn around and go get Haley? She'd chosen to help him escape. Going back would only mean his capture. And he knew that his mission was bigger than either of them. But that knowledge didn't change the recognition that something had changed inside him. He wasn't ready to give up everything for the mission anymore. He still believed in the importance of his duty, but his responsibility to see her safe now seemed more urgent. Ryan sped on as inside himself an internal battle raged.

HALEY WATCHED IN shock as Ryan sped away from her.

She prayed that he reached the target before his competition. She did not know what was on that flash drive. Only that it was classified, stolen intelligence and that men were ready to kill and die to obtain it.

She'd given him his shot, taken a risk. She'd provided him the location of the flash drive and created the diversion that allowed him to escape. One that might land her in jail. What had she been thinking? Had she lost her mind? The only thing that might kill her mother quicker than losing another child was seeing her only surviving child go to prison.

But she knew she would do it again, if given the chance. She was no longer that fearful young woman who had set off for adventure camp. Her time with Ryan had forged her into something tough and selfless and, yes, brave.

The female officer stared down at her from the controls of the boat.

"You are in a lot of trouble, ma'am."

Haley gave a rueful smile. "Don't I know it."

"Grab the towline," she said, tossing Haley a rope. Once she had a hold the officer hauled her in and then picked up her radio, reporting two fugitives.

Haley was assisted on board the police vessel and handcuffed before being deposited on the rear bench of the craft. A second vessel arrived with a blue flashing light affixed to the bow and Marine Police emblazoned on the side. It sped past them toward the spot they had left their stranded attacker.

Haley was taken to the marina and efficiently arrested, read her rights and escorted off the dock. Her first arrest and every tourist with a camera phone was there to witness her humiliation.

Along the road were vehicles from the New York State Police office, the sheriff's office, local village law enforcement professionals and one from Fish and Wildlife.

Haley burned with embarrassment as she was transferred to the back of a police unit. She was shivering and soaking wet, leaving a puddle on the floor mats behind the wire mesh that separated the front from the back of the patrol car.

Once at the station she endured the intake procedure including fingerprinting, breathalyzer and a swab for gunpowder residue. Then she was placed in a cell and the door firmly locked.

She had stopped shivering and her tank top was nearly dry before anyone appeared to check on her.

"I want to speak to a lawyer," she said.

"I'll bet you do. But right now we are transferring your custody to federal authorities. Drug enforcement agents are en route. They seem very anxious to speak to you."

"I need to speak to your chief of police."

"No lawyer?"

"No."

"All right then." The young officer departed and returned with a woman in her middle years, plain clothes in business casual, her hair dyed an unnatural shade of red that clashed with her lipstick.

"You wanted to speak to me?"

Haley didn't know what she expected a small-town police chief to look like, but this wasn't it.

"Chief?"

She nodded. "You want to make a statement?"

"No, I want to tell you that the agents who are coming for me are not with the Drug Enforcement Agency. They're imposters."

"And you know this…how?"

"They're foreign agents posing as US officials. They tried to kill us."

Haley could tell how well her story was going by the chief's expression, which went from startled to something that might have been pity.

"The guy from the lake. He's one of them."

The chief's brow quirked.

"Where is he?" asked Haley.

"The one man we pulled out of the water has a bruised trachea. I released him to seek medical attention, but before, he presented me with his ID. He's a Kingston police officer."

"He's not. He tried to shoot me."

"Why would men, posing as law enforcement, be after you?"

"Not me, but the man who I was with."

"You mean the armed fugitive who left you behind after he stole the officer's Jet Ski?"

Haley bit her lip. "Can you just keep me here and not let them take me?"

The chief pressed her lips together as she shook her head. "Much as I'd like to toss you into one of our very fine jail cells, it seems I'm outranked. Even if I wanted to keep you, and I do, but not for your benefit, I have no choice."

"Can you at least confirm they are who they say they are?" asked Haley.

The woman's brow wrinkled. "First, that's just protocol and second, are you really telling me how to do my job right now?" She turned to the officer beside her. "We're done. Get her some dry clothing, courtesy of the village of Lake George."

RYAN FELT AN ache in his stomach as he left Haley behind. She deserved better. Should he waste the advantage she had given him or heed her wishes?

He didn't usually have such conflicting emotions. The mission came first, above everything up to and including his life. Or it had. Now he tried to think of a way to make this right.

Once he completed his delivery and spoke to his supervisors, Haley would be freed from any charges the locals might want to slap on her. If he could complete it and recover what Takashi had hidden before his competition figured out the clue.

He thought of the agent reading the note, if it were even possible after it was soaked in lake water. Assuming his competition couldn't decipher it or was unable to gain any useful information, what would be his next move?

It should be to go after the thumb drive, but if he didn't know where to look…

Haley!

He had to go back for her, right now, before the flash drive. Before anything else.

It wasn't just about the big picture. It was about the little picture, the one that involved keeping Haley alive and seeing if she could forgive him for doing what she had asked instead of what was best for her.

If he didn't get there first, they'd pick her up and…

Ryan thought of his short time in their captivity as he ran the Jet Ski up onto the lakeshore and took off running.

He had to get to her before they did.

HALEY SAT IN a chair across from the chief in an interrogation room. Her hands were secured before her in handcuffs and she held them still to keep the metal from rattling when she spoke. The chief sat before an open laptop across from her, as she went over Haley's statement again. The chief was interested in specifics, details that could verify some of what she claimed or catch her in a lie.

There was a knock and a young officer stepped through the door.

"DEA officers are here with a van to take custody."

Haley's eyes widened. "You can't let me go with them."

The chief ignored her, still looking at her computer. "That was fast."

Haley stood up and backed away from the table. The chief spoke to her officer. "Bring them on back."

The young man stepped out and the door closed.

"It's not them. You can't release me." Haley was babbling. She knew it but couldn't seem to stop.

The chief lifted a hand.

The young officer appeared again, holding the door as two men in plain clothes stepped in. She recognized the beefy one immediately. He was the one from the cabin and also the accident.

"Hornet," she said.

He did not even glance her way.

She lifted her joined hands, pointing a finger at the large muscular man whose shoulders stretched the suit fabric.

"That's him. He's the one from the crash. They called him Hornet and that one is Needle," she said, pointing at the shorter, balding man with light brown skin. "I hit him with my thermos. He has a scar or scab up here." She placed two fingers on the crown of her own head.

Needle ignored her and spoke to the chief. "You have the release papers?"

The chief nodded and nudged a clipboard on the table in his direction.

"You guys work out of Albany?"

He nodded and scrawled his signature on the form.

"I have a cousin down there. I think I'll just give him a call."

She extracted her phone from a side pocket of her blazer and glanced away to enter the pass code. That was why she didn't see Hornet draw his knife. He stepped forward and punched multiple holes in the chief's torso.

Haley screamed.

Chapter Eighteen

Blood welled up on the chief's clean white blouse as she dropped to her knees, the phone sliding from her hand and clattering to the floor.

Hornet seized Haley's arm and dragged her out. The young officer stepped into the hall before them.

"Everything all right?" he asked.

"Just fine," said Hornet.

"He just killed your chief," Haley shouted. "Go look!"

The young man's hand went to his pistol but he just stood there as she was dragged past him followed by Needle.

"Quiet," said Hornet, propelling her out of the secure area, into the hall that led to the street and to the waiting black SUV. Needle waited by the exit, preparing, she supposed, to cover their escape.

By now they should have discovered the chief. Would she survive so many puncture wounds? Haley's entire body felt cold and her legs had turned to wood.

Hornet jostled her to his side as he opened the rear sliding door of the black GMC Terrain. She glanced into the SUV's interior and looked down the barrel of a gun. Her gaze flashed to the gunman, turned sideways in the driver's seat, and recognized Ryan.

Her captor noticed just a fraction of a second later. It was enough time for her to step away from Hornet and him to try, unsuccessfully, to draw his pistol.

Ryan fired and Hornet fell backward to his seat as his shot went through the metal step beyond the sliding door.

"Get in!" Ryan shouted. "He's wearing body armor."

Haley scrambled through the opening.

"There are two of them," she said as Hornet grasped her ankle. She glanced to Ryan, who held his gun aimed toward their attackers, clearly unable to get in another shot. Haley spun on her seat and kicked with her free foot. Hornet released her and she scrambled into the vehicle, not stopping as she was rocked from side to side when Ryan took off. Needle ran at them from across the wide sidewalk. The sliding door slid half closed and banged open as she dove headfirst over the central console dividing the two front seats.

"You came back," she said, her voice breathless.

"Are you hit?"

She checked herself, but it was hard to see past the specks of white light flashing before her eyes.

"I don't think so."

Was she going to faint? She righted herself in the passenger seat and lowered her head to her palms. The handcuffs slid farther down her wrists.

"They got escaping armed gunman on that adventure list?" he asked.

She was looking back at the way they had come, breathless and gasping.

"He stabbed the chief. He hit her multiple times. We have to call for help."

"She's in a police station. They are in the same building as paramedics and fire rescue. If she's alive, she's got the best care anyone could hope for."

"Where are we going?"

"I'm going after the flash drive," said Ryan.

"You don't have it yet?" She blinked at him in astonishment. Did she understand that he'd come after her first?

"Go!" she said and thumped the dashboard for good measure.

RYAN SET OFF toward the highway where the village dropped away and a water park, amusement park, ice-cream stand and two eighteen-hole miniature golf courses awaited.

They had to hurry. Collect his package, contact the Company and set up an extraction operation. After that, he needed to get them both into safe hands.

Since his last attempt to contact his handler had coincided with his cover being blown, he was suspicious of the lines of communication. He decided to use the safe number, following a well-ordered protocol.

They reached the miniature golf spot, leaving the Terrain parked in the lot between a minivan and a hybrid wagon with a rubber raft tied to the roof. He and Haley collected two putters from the stand and waited by the exit for a family who had completed their round and were still arguing over a hole as Ryan and Haley slipped past them. Together they sauntered in the opposite direction around the holes as if in no hurry at all. Haley was a natural, if you overlooked the trembling hands. She blended in perfectly among the tourists here.

They moved past the families at each hole until they reached the one with the enormous yellow sombrero. Then Haley pretended to be lining up her shot. Even without a ball she was convincing. Meanwhile, he circled the sombrero.

"Honey?" she called. "Is there a hole or anything I have to hit through?"

He inspected the exterior, looking for the possible hiding spot. He noticed an electrical box near the bottom at the back. Once the group of three moved on, he stepped onto the wrinkled, worn green carpet and behind the cement representation of the iconic hat. He flipped open the cover of the box and found nothing.

HE SHOOK HIS HEAD. Haley stepped forward and checked, locating the flash drive taped to the roof of the junction box above the groupings of wires.

She gripped the drive in her fist and turned to Ryan, elation racing in her blood with the adrenaline.

"You got it?" he asked.

She nodded, unable to hold back the grin as she showed him.

He laughed and then lifted her at the waist, turning her in a circle before letting her drop into his waiting arms.

The kiss was quick and joyful. But the celebration

ended when Ryan stiffened and glanced around. They were drawing notice of the families on the mini golf course. He released her and they headed back to the GMC.

"I have to contact my handlers," Ryan said.

"But you said they are compromised. They might be the ones who sent those men after us."

"I have friends. I can get the information to the right people."

"You have someone that you trust with your life?"

"I have lots of people I trust with my life, including you. But I only have one person I trust with *your* life."

"Who's that?"

"My old commanding officer and the man who recruited me. Colonel Jorge L. Hernandez. He's retired but I know he can get me help. We need to get to a phone."

Ryan opened the door for her and she slipped inside. As he backed out, she popped the flash drive into the USB port in the navigation system and pressed Copy. He drove them to a motel as she uploaded the information into the vehicle's hard drive.

The motel he chose was the sort of place that fell between classically charming and seriously behind the times. The two-story L-shaped building had balconies with those bright metal vintage chairs in various colors and hanging baskets of flowers that cascaded blossoms. Each door was painted a different color.

They did not pull to the office but drove past the pool full of children splashing and parents relaxing in lounge chairs. He chose a spot at the end of the line of cars that already filled the lot. Then he parked and left the SUV. She slipped the drive out of the USB port and offered it to him when he rounded the vehicle.

"Could you tell what's on there?" he asked. Clearly he had not realized that she'd copied the drive.

Should she tell him?

"I couldn't read it. But the…" But the navigation system had. "That brand of auto has something called a—"

He cut her off. "No time now," he said. "Tell me later."

She followed him to a downstairs room.

"How are you going to get in?"

In answer he lifted his hand and knocked. They waited in silence and when there was no response to his second try, he pressed his shoulder to the door and pushed. The door swung inward, taking a piece of the frame with it.

"I'll never rent a room in a place like this again," she said.

He clasped her elbow and hurried her inside, closing the door behind them and using the chain to keep it closed.

The room was littered with suitcases that seemed to have been mauled by animals, judging from the clothing and personal belongings that spewed forth.

He moved to the bed and made his call, reversing the charges. She listened as he explained their situation to someone—she assumed it was his colonel—with Spartan efficiency, leaving out all the terror and blood and death that had recently surrounded them. Haley sank down on the end of the queen-size bed, exhaustion suddenly taking her.

There was silence as he listened, presumably to the colonel's instructions. She heard him return the handset to the cradle. He touched her arm, startling her from her stupor. She lifted her chin from her chest and their eyes met.

"Takashi is safe and out of the country. He made it to Toronto. Hernandez said they are still investigating the breach but it definitely wasn't on our end."

"That's good news." Her brow furrowed. "So those two women, the hikers, were lying about capturing him?"

"Yes. If he left the country, they could assume he had made his drop. That made me the only one who would know where to find it."

He rummaged through the piles of clothing on the dresser and chair, pausing occasionally to check the size of a shirt. Then he stripped. The sight of his broad back brought her brain back into focus and got her heart thumping, as well.

She tucked the image of him half-naked away for later use and smiled. Best thing that had happened all day, next to surviving with their lives.

Ryan shrugged into a thin button-up shirt in a check, the sort used by fisherman to keep the sun off their backs. Then he dropped his cargo pants and stepped into navy blue shorts. They were the sort with multiple pockets that dads wore on vacation. On Ryan, they gave a completely different look. He continued to sift through the things.

"You ever shop in a conventional store?" she asked.

He grinned at her. "Your turn. What about this?" He held up a red sundress.

She stood. "I can try."

Haley took hers to the bathroom. The dress had spaghetti straps and a V-neck. The size was right and the fabric was spandex so it clung to her torso and hips. When she returned she had the satisfaction of seeing his eyes bulge.

"Holy smokes! That looks good on you." He lifted a pair of sandals. "Will these work?"

"For walking, not running."

"We are walking out of here and tomorrow we'll have transport."

"This dress makes me look like a target."

"It will definitely make me invisible."

She grinned. "So I'm your…"

"Diversion." He grinned, coming to put his hands on her waist and turning her slightly from side to side. "No bad angle."

She met his gaze and her smile dropped away. The intensity, the sheer heat of that look, melted her.

"This is stealing," she said.

"It's called commandeering," he answered.

She felt only mildly guilty as Ryan tossed a spray deodorant, comb and toothpaste into a small carry-on suitcase.

"Ready?" he asked.

"Where are we going?"

"My friend got us a room at the Gideon."

She whistled. "Swank."

"You know it?" he asked.

"It's in Saratoga Spa State Park. We used to drive past it on the way to SPAC."

"SPAC?"

"Saratoga Performing Arts Center. We would go to SPAC for concerts. It's an outdoor amphitheater. Just great. Anyway, we would drive through the park. Dad always made us stop to drink the water and…" She looked away.

"And…" he encouraged.

When she turned back her eyes were glittering as water tested her lower lids but she went on.

"Maggie always went first and said how sweet it was, and bubbly. Then I'd drink, as if I didn't know what was coming and make a big show of how terrible it tasted." The tears fell in unison and rolled down her cheeks.

"Sulfur?" he said.

"Yup. Every time. Hard to believe that folks came, still come, to taste the waters."

"To bathe in them."

"Yes, but to drink them, too. They used to bottle it and sell it. It's naturally carbonated. But the wells, groundwater I guess, got too low and the state stepped in. You know it's the only natural geyser east of the Mississippi?"

"How do you know?"

"Dad. He loves New York State history. The Revolutionary War is his bailiwick."

"Now there's a good old word." He extended the handle of the carry-on and then offered his elbow. "Shall we?"

He paused at the open cement staircase just past the ice and vending machines.

She glanced longingly at the display of cold drinks. Why didn't she realize how thirsty she was until right now?

"Want something?"

"I don't have any money."

He reached in his pocket and pulled out several bills, then fed them into the machine. She knew where he'd gotten that cash and hesitated.

"Oh, take it."

"Will you find that family and reimburse them?"

He sighed and then nodded. "Yes. Okay. Now pick something."

"Police will be here over that break-in."

"Yup. And we will be long gone." He motioned for her to continue before him to their vehicle. Once there, he held open the door for her. *Must be the dress*, she thought and climbed into the seat.

"Do you think the police caught Hornet and Needle and… Was there another one?"

"There was." His smile was chilling. It reminded her that they were not out on a date to the fanciest place in town, but fleeing hired killers. And Ryan, he was one of the good guys, but that smile seemed to indicate he enjoyed his job a bit too much for her liking. What was she even doing here with him?

Why had he come back? It made no sense.

"Why did you come back for me before you collected the flash drive?"

His knuckles flexed on the wheel.

"You saved me. Just returning the favor."

"Favor or obligation?"

"What?"

"I'm wondering if I am like one of your men. Your responsibility. The ones back there that you said trusted you to keep them alive. I'm like them."

He shook his head, but his jaw was clamped tight.

"You ever work with a partner?" she asked.

He glared at her and then returned his attention to the road.

"Have a long-term relationship since coming home?"

"What are you, my shrink?"

"Did you have one of those?"

He stared out the windshield. "A few. It's required on occasion after fieldwork."

"Well, I've had more than a few. After my sister's death they introduced me to something called survivor's guilt. I've spent enough time talking about my guilt to wonder if maybe you are burying yours behind a revolving door of dangerous assignments."

He hit the brakes and they swerved to the shoulder of the road. Haley was tossed forward and then backward into the seat.

"Spit it out, Haley. Stop poking at me like a piñata. What kind of guilt we talking here?"

She swiveled in her seat to meet his glare. "It occurs to me that the risks you take might have something to do with your feelings over the men you could not save. People die in wars, Ryan. Good people, and not you nor anyone else can prevent that. Putting yourself in situations where you could die might not be so much about feeling alive as not feeling at fault."

"You take psychology along with those computer coding classes?"

"Well, what do you think?"

"I think I couldn't bring them back. Getting killed now won't change that."

But it would remove his pain, she thought.

"True enough."

"So if you're done, I have to deliver that thumb drive and get back to base."

"Certainly."

They drove back along the main drag toward the town of Saratoga Springs but cut off the highway before reaching the place she could see perfectly in her mind's eye—Union Avenue, with the entrance to the racetrack that was the destination in August of each year. Past that, closer to town on the wide, tree-lined street, sat the grand old Victorian homes with generous front porches often only used during the summer season. They ended at Congress Park where mineral waters still flowed from marble water fountain. Instead, they took the less scenic back way to the Gideon Putnam down South Broadway and into Saratoga Spa State Park.

The long elegant drive gave impressive views of the large brick resort and spa fronted with multiple columns and a green awning. The entrance to the Gideon Putnam was magnificent, dressed in a profusion of planted blooms bursting from the garden beds that lined the path. Enormous flower baskets sagged, spilling over with purple-and-white blossoms. They pulled up to the columns that marked the hotel's entrance here inside the state park.

Ryan left the car with the valet and opened her door, offering a hand as she slipped from the vehicle. Then he retrieved "their" carry-on and escorted her inside. His hand was warm and steady. Meanwhile she was trembling again as she wondered if their attackers had followed them here.

She could not keep her head from swiveling at the lux lobby for potential threats. As they continued along, she took in the Oriental carpet, warm rust-colored walls and large cascading flower arrangements set on period tables. They followed the carpet runner past the flanking columns.

"Been inside before?" he asked.

"Only to the Sunday brunch, which is awesome."

"We'll have to come back sometime, after you finish adventure camp."

"I think I'm done with adventure camp," she said.

"No cliff jumping or zip-lining?"

"Pass," she said.

"That's what you would have said about all of the challenges."

"Right now, I'm nervous about the challenge of checking in."

He squeezed her hand and cast her a smile that was meant to reassure but instead set off a current of electricity that seemed to lift every hair on her body. Now she was picturing him naked again.

At the registration desk, Ryan took on a very convincing Midwestern accent, told the customer service agent that this was their first trip to the area and gave a name she had never heard of.

"Mr. and Mrs. Terry Greenbrier."

After a few seconds that stretched to eternity, the young man smiled and nodded.

"Yes, I have you both in a porch suite."

Mr. Greenbrier turned to his missus and gave her a chiding look.

"Honey, a suite?"

"Oh, you'll love it," said the receptionist, coming to her rescue. "French doors leading out to a private enclosed porch with views of the state park. We also have a free shuttle to the racetrack, downtown and the casino."

"Hmm," he said, seeming to consider. "Sounds good. Do you have a business center?"

They did.

"We also have two pools on-site and complimentary use of the historic Roosevelt Baths & Spa." He continued tapping on his console and his brows lifted. "I have a package waiting for you. If you will just give me one minute."

He disappeared in a back room returning with a priority box. "Here you are, Mr. Greenbrier. Two keys?"

"Yes, and I'd like to order room service."

"Our kitchen is open until ten p.m." He sent two keys into the system, loading the information to open their doors.

"Wonderful," said Ryan, accepting the keys and box.

Directions were given and Ryan led her to the elevators for a short one-floor trip to their room.

"Will you transmit the thumb drive data in the business center?" Haley asked.

"Orders are to collect and deliver." He opened the box and extracted a phone, identification cards, credit cards and cash.

"Aren't you at all curious?" she asked.

He gave her a hard look. "No."

"I could probably see what's on there. Might be time sensitive."

He shook his head. Was that because of orders or because he still didn't trust her? Haley fumed at that possibility.

He handed her an Illinois license with her photo and the name Irene Greenbrier upon it. Her jaw dropped.

"Handy," she said. "Who from?"

"Compliments of Colonel Hernandez again."

"So if he can send this, why can't he send more agents?"

"They'll be along, as soon as he gets to my CO."

The elevator stopped on the second floor and they stepped from the car. Haley consulted the signage and saw the word Spa.

"Trapped in a deluxe hotel with potential chance of spa treatment. That's my kind of adventure camp."

He smiled at that.

"You have the cash. But I don't have word that our attackers have been apprehended. So for now, you stick close to me."

That did not sound like punishment. In fact, it raised all kinds of possibilities.

He let her into the room and then followed, throwing the dead bolt. Then Ryan walked to the window and checked for an escape route. The ground below was grassy and faced the tall pines in the state park. Then he turned to face Haley, who flicked on a light on the desk. He closed the curtains, removing them as potential targets.

"Hungry?" he asked.

"Starving."

Ryan lifted the phone. "What would you like?"

"Anything?"

"Courtesy of Uncle."

"Steak, steak fries, salad with French dressing and their best-selling dessert."

"Which is?"

"Who cares? It will be wonderful."

"Coffee?"

"Red wine," she answered.

He nodded and placed her order and his, asking for their meal to be delivered at eight. *Ninety minutes*, she thought, wondering what he planned to do in the meantime.

She had her hopes. Desires, really.

When he lowered the receiver, she was within easy reach. He leaned in, his hand going to her lower back as he gave her a kiss that she thought was meant to be a quick goodbye. But his mouth was gentle and she stepped closer. He tugged her against him as he deepened the kiss. His fingers delved into her hair and she gave herself over to the kiss.

Ryan drew back at last, giving her a look of speculation.

"Don't blame me," she said. "You started it."

"Looking forward to finishing it even more," he said.

"Why wait?"

His jaw dropped. Did he wonder if this was the same timid mouse who didn't like to take chances? Dressed in red, her daring finally matched her attire.

"Why, indeed."

Chapter Nineteen

Ryan walked her back to the queen-size bed. The moment they made contact with the mattress, Haley fell back onto the satin coverlet. Ryan controlled her descent.

Haley responded to the pressure of his hips pushing her to the bedding, arcing to increase the contact. They were safe and he was here with her. She knew the woman who had driven her rental car to an adventure camp in which she never intended to participate would consider all possible consequences of sleeping with Ryan again. That Haley would worry about what sort of messages this behavior would send to him. And ultimately she would do the responsible thing, which was also the safest thing. She'd tell him to stop.

But that woman was gone forever. She tugged him down for a greedy kiss. Their mouths slashed across each other's in a rough and hungry taking of pleasure. The contact caused her skin to pucker, increasing the need building inside her like floodwater against a dam.

He pulled away to catch his breath, pressing his forehead to hers as he used one hand to cradle her head.

"Haley, are you sure about this?"

"Yes. Are you?"

There was a flicker of hesitancy that made her open her eyes. He lifted his chin, gazing back at her.

"So much it hurts," he said.

Her smile was slow and seemed to curl inside her whole body. His kisses began at her temple and moved south. By the time he reached her hips he had slid her dress all the way down and off her body, unwrapping her like a cherished gift.

He held her dress in his fist and made a show of dropping it. She giggled and then tugged at his checked dad shirt.

"Your turn."

The man was graceful as a dancer, removing the shirt with the sweep of a single hand. Next he stood to unfasten the belt and rivet closing his shorts. In a moment he stepped from the last of his clothing, leaving nothing to her imagination.

Oh how she wished she had a photographic memory.

She crooked her finger. "Come here."

He did, eventually. But he made several stops along the way. So by the time his lips again met hers, she had already experienced exactly how shattering that mouth could be.

She let her knees drop to the bedding, so thankful for all those hours of tae kwon do stretches. Ryan nestled against her and she guided him home, watching the pleasure break across his face as he inched deeper and deeper inside her.

Then she lifted her hips and discovered that even former Marines, who were seasoned agents, had a breaking point.

HALEY WOKE TO hear the shower running. She lifted her head from the coverlet and listened as the water flipped off. Billowing steam preceded his return to the room.

The white towel around his waist and the picture he presented had her grinning up at him. The broad muscular chest and the corded muscles of his stomach made her mouth go dry as other parts of her went all dewy. In his hand, he carried one of the hotel's white terrycloth robes.

"Oh, no. Don't look at me like that," he chided. "Or I'll tell them to cancel dinner."

He opened the robe to her. She slipped from between the linens and stood before him, giving him time to take a good long look. He lifted the robe a few inches and cleared his throat.

"Haley, you're killing me."

Their eyes met and the electric current surged between them. She gripped the plush collar of the robe he held and used it to tug him closer for a kiss just as a knock came at the door.

"Phooey," she said and shrugged into the robe, cinching the belt with unnecessary force.

Ryan went to the door and she trailed him. It was not until he was checking through the peephole that she saw the grip of a handgun peeking out the top of his towel at the center of his back.

He opened the door and allowed the server to carry the tray to the balcony where a small table waited. Haley thought that this spot would be a lovely place for breakfast, but at night, with the curtains closed, it was less appealing.

But with those blackout curtains, they also would present less of a target. Maybe she was getting the hang of this.

Ryan remained in the bedroom area and signed the bill he was presented with one hand. The other was now in a terry pocket of his robe, likely gripping the handgun. The server thanked him three times on the way out, so she suspected Ryan had added a generous tip to the bill.

When he joined her on the balcony, the hotel robe covered the swath of naked chest that had been a complete distraction.

Only the smell of steak could have lured her away.

"When did we last eat?" she asked.

"Sunday night at the Wellers' apartment."

"Yesterday? No wonder I'm starving."

Ryan removed the silver covers from their plates and opened her mini ketchup bottle. Conversation lagged as they tucked into their meals. In most instances, she could not or would not have eaten all her fries, but she finished them and every leaf of lettuce in her salad and every bite of steak. She slowed down only after she finished the last of the carafe of wine and eyed the desserts. Ryan had ordered two.

"They said the red velvet cake, with cream cheese frosting and toasted walnuts, is most popular and the mint mousse on a chocolate brownie and ganache is also a top seller."

"Hmm," she hummed and went for the mousse, which was an electric green.

Ryan took the cake and sliced off a third and then set the plate back before her. She gave it her very best effort, but could not finish both. Ryan came to the rescue and cleaned up the remains.

"Would you like anything else?" he asked.

"A shower?"

"That's a great idea. I have to do some business. So you go ahead."

"Oh, okay." Did she sound disappointed? She didn't want to seem needy. Ryan lifted the tray and carried it out.

She followed him as far as the hallway. On his return he flipped on the phone.

"Can you believe it?" he said, staring at the phone. "It's not set up."

"I can do it," she said. He gave her the phone and she began the simple steps to get it working. Then she modified the settings, changed the ringtone and turned on the tracking function. Finally, she added herself as a user.

"Pass code?" she asked.

"1399," he said, absently as he buttoned up his shirt and cinched the belt. She handed back his phone.

"You have four messages."

Only then did he pause to smile at her. She got the feeling he was waiting for her to leave before conducting his business.

She headed into the bathroom. There she paused to

lean against the closed door. She was alone and safe. The wonderful meal made her feel relaxed and drowsy. She had just enough steam left to wash herself. She didn't really want him to join her in the shower. Did she?

The shower's adjustable spray head was exactly what she needed, massaging her tired muscles and turning her skin a healthy pink. A few moments later, she stepped to the mat and used two fluffy towels. One for her body and one for her hair.

Ryan knocked and then slipped open the door, offering her a women's bathroom kit complete with comb, toothpaste and a toothbrush.

She kissed him and he smiled. "Steamy," he said and stroked her cheek.

"How's it going?" she asked.

His smile remained, but his hand slipped away. "See you when you finish."

Not an answer, she realized.

Haley clutched the bounty he'd provided and used every single product. She dried herself in the plush terry and wrapped an oversize towel about herself before combing her hair.

She took a moment for a critical check of her reflection. She looked dewy and fresh and appealing. She found Ryan sitting up in bed with a mountain of pillows behind his bare torso. The phone's screen glowed, highlighting his cheeks and deepening the dark, tempting hollows of his chest and abdomen.

He glanced up and smiled.

"Wow. And I thought nothing could look better than that red dress."

"You prefer the towel?" she asked.

"I prefer neither." He set aside the phone and flipped back the covers, giving her an eyeful. Apparently Ryan also slept in the nude.

And suddenly, sleep was the furthest thing from her mind.

RYAN OPENED HIS eyes in the still, dark hotel room. The darkness was artificial, provided by the blackout curtains, judging from the bright sunlight that stole below the window coverings.

The sense of unease returned and he swallowed against the regret. He was used to trouble and danger, but not this kind. Haley was the kind of trouble he could not handle because she distracted him and made him think about things he had no business wanting—like a future with her.

Was she right that his father had lived a meaningful life and that had been more important than a meaningful death? He'd never really thought of it that way. He had only seen what his father had missed, a chance to make a difference, an opportunity to see the world and a vital mission to complete.

But as he lay with Haley in his arms, he thought of his mother and father. His parents had been in love. They had showed it in a million different acts of caring. Why had he forgotten about that? Perhaps those loving acts had been more valuable than the illusion he chased. The mission was important and he'd sworn to complete it, if he could. Everything was in place to ensure the transport of the thumb drive. After it was gone, he'd have no reason to stay with Haley.

She shifted in her sleep, stroking his chest. Her hair fanned his shoulder and her clean, inviting scent reached him. He sighed, knowing he would miss her and knowing that the best thing he could do for Haley Nobel was to disappear from her life.

He was not the right man for her. She wanted a stable, reliable guy who was likely to come home to her. He couldn't even count the close calls he'd had in the past year. Too darn many. What would his parents say? Would they be proud of him or disappointed?

His parents would have liked Haley.

Haley was a good woman. And he was throwing her away.

Ryan shifted, slipping from her arms. Haley rolled to her back, breathing softly. He glanced at the clock, which told him it was nearly seven in the morning. Time to get moving. He had a meeting at nine.

Before settling in last night he had used the paper door-hanger menu to order breakfast and hung it outside the door. The food should be arriving in about thirty minutes.

He gave a reluctant look back at Haley, wanting to make love to her, stay with her, and that he just could not do. He had orders but he could at least feed her before he said goodbye.

Ryan showered and dressed. He was just wiping the shaving cream off his face when the knock came at the door. He held the handgun as he checked the porter through the peephole and then told him to wait. The man called for him to take his time in his response but rolled his eyes.

Ryan glanced at Haley, who was now sitting up in bed.

"Everything okay?" she asked.

Chapter Twenty

Haley's voice was low and husky and so appealing his throat went dry and his body hardened instantly. Did she know the picture she made, wrapped in a sheet, her hair tousled and her lips still swollen from their lovemaking?

"Breakfast," he said.

She nodded and slipped from the bed, naked. He tracked her as she strode to the bathroom, not making a show of her perfect body, but not hiding it, either. Was this the same woman who he'd met on the highway?

It wasn't. She'd changed and now she was exactly the sort of woman his mother would approve of.

Where had that come from?

The door clicked shut and Ryan admitted the porter. The food was set on the porch and Ryan showed him out, adding a tip to his bill. Back on the porch, Ryan swept open the curtains and opened the French doors. He had one hour before his meet. He had his first cup of coffee while waiting for Haley.

It was worth the wait. She appeared twenty minutes later in a turquoise tennis outfit that appeared to be one piece. Her slim, pale feet were bare and her hair was pulled back, but wet.

"Good morning," he rose to kiss her lightly on the lips and then offered her a chair.

She perched on the edge and cast him a welcoming smile. "Smells wonderful."

"Coffee?"

Haley nodded and then began exploring beneath the silver covers revealing eggs, fried potatoes, sausage, ham, bacon, a basket of bagels and muffins, strawberry crepes and fresh raspberries.

"Holy smokes! What a feast."

"Eat up."

He served her eggs and bacon with potatoes. She also tried the crepe and part of a cranberry muffin.

"The coffee is excellent. Everything is excellent." She beamed at him and he felt like a heel. Under other circumstances, she would have woken in an empty bed. Maybe his old method was easier. Easier for him, at least. He managed to tuck away the eggs and ham, but wasn't very hungry. He wished he could bring her along. But he had orders. She was to be abandoned at this hotel to find her own means back to her old life.

Would she miss him at all?

"Wow, am I full."

He smiled. "You deserve a good meal after all I've put you through."

"Well, what was the alternative?"

His smile faltered. "I was going to leave you behind."

She frowned. "At the adventure camp?"

His hesitation made her wonder if he'd considered leaving her more than once. It also made her realize that this would be a really excellent place to leave her. They were momentarily safe. He had arranged to deliver the thumb drive this morning and once that was done, his mission would be complete.

He wouldn't need to protect her any longer. His expression told her she guessed correctly. What she had seen as the beginning of a relationship, he had seen as the final curtain before pulling a disappearing act.

She'd never find him. She knew that much.

"Haley, I thought about what you said. About the possibility of time-sensitive information on that drive. Takashi moved the meet here, I'm wondering if there was a reason beyond pursuit by the group he hacked. I want to check the data on the flash drive, as you suggested."

"Is it protected?" she asked.

"I have no idea." He stared down at the device in question. "Do you think you can read it?"

"Almost definitely," she said.

"What if it is a trigger for some virus or terrorist attack?" he asked.

"Then we should know that. I won't be connected to the internet when I check it. Worst case, it damages the computer."

"All right. I'll call the desk and ask to borrow a laptop."

He did and they waited for the delivery.

"You don't trust very many people, do you?" she asked.

"Very few."

She smiled and poured a final cup of coffee for them as they waited. The knock signaled the delivery.

Ryan checked the peephole then opened the door, gun in one hand as he accepted the computer with the other. He brought her the laptop and drive.

"No Wi-Fi," he said.

"Of course." She went to work, booting up, accessing the drive and finally flicking open files.

"I'm not sure what I'm seeing. Looks like doubles of each file." She opened the doubles.

The coffee in his mug had gone cold by the time she lifted her head and grinned.

"All right, here we go."

He moved his chair around to sit beside her.

"Here's the index," she pointed. "I had some trouble because it's not in English. Kanji. Japanese characters. But this is an identical index inside the first one. It's the translations."

She studied the screen. "This one is a chemical formula, something biologic."

Ryan straightened. "How do you know that?"

"I was premed for a while. I took biochemistry. Loved it, really."

"Huh?" he said, glancing at her as if she was some alien species.

"I'm not sure what it is. I can check online with the phone."

"No Wi-Fi," he said. "That search could alert interested parties."

"Fine." She clicked open another file and glanced

his way. "You want me to back up this drive onto this computer?"

"No. No copies."

She shrugged and her mouth twitched as she returned her attention back to the laptop.

"This one is marked Siming's Army. This one says Vaccine," she said, pointing to the two files. "This one is labeled Dosage."

"Open Vaccine," he said.

She did. "It's handling instructions and…this part gives dates and times for delivery."

"Location?"

"Not that I can see on this file."

"When?"

"Soon, a few weeks."

"Here's one marked Storage. I thought it was file storage, but…" She clicked open a series of folders. "Transport orders, care instructions and delivery address," she read. She opened the document and her hands slid from the keyboard. Her mouth gaped as she pointed with one finger. "New York. Here. Look at the location. That's in the Adirondacks."

"That's why Takashi moved the meet. Why he insisted I have a team in place. He wanted to get me closer to the shipment."

"Likely. The only location that I did find is a garnet mine outside Lake George. It says they have the serum for participants."

"Serum?" asked Ryan.

"My guess is that is either a vaccine or an antidote to some biological toxin. If you are launching a biological weaponized disease, you would want your people protected."

"I have to go there."

"Now?"

"Yes, now, before our adversaries recover it."

"By yourself?"

"I'll contact Colonel Braiser."

"Who is he?"

"Friend of a friend."

"You trust him?"

"My former commanding officer, Jorge Hernandez, vouches for him. I have to go with that."

"So you'll wait for Braiser and your people to arrive and then join them?"

He didn't answer.

"Wait. No. Not by yourself. You said that your people are coming. They could be here in…what? An hour or two."

"I don't know when they will be here, but I know where I am and where the biological weapon is."

"You have no idea how it's guarded," she said.

"I have no choice."

She blinked at him. "I'm sorry I told you."

He stood.

"Haley, you need to go."

"Go where?"

"Back to your old life."

But she didn't want to. Now she saw her Brooklyn apartment as what it was, a safe little cave in which to hide. And her job…taking no risks as she broke down virtual walls.

She stood and moved to the window, touched the curtain, and he was there, clasping her wrist, drawing her away. She would make a fine target in that window for anyone searching from the woods. Were they out there now?

"I should come with you," she said.

His eyes were sad as he gave a shake of his head. "I won't bring you back into danger. You saved my life. I've tried to do the same."

The debt was repaid. She let her chin sink to her chest, wishing she could go back and never have spent the night in his arms. Because how could she let him go, now that she knew the perfection of his body, their lovemaking and oh, dear Lord, she loved him. The tears dribbled down her cheeks. She dashed them away.

What an idiot she was.

"How do you know they won't come after me?" she asked. "That I'm really safe?"

She didn't care if she was safe as long as she was with him and so she grasped at straws.

"Once I make the delivery, you are of zero value to them."

And to him. She looked up into his eyes and saw regret.

He released her wrist and stepped back, letting his hands drop to his sides. He was letting her go. She had no doubt.

She wanted to ask him to come back to her and suddenly saw herself through his eyes. She'd mainly been a hindrance, making his job harder on several occasions.

Going with him now could endanger him even further and nothing she could say would stop him.

"Well, thank you for keeping me alive," she said. Her voice broke.

"Oh, Haley, you're killing me." He dragged her in and tucked her close. He stroked her hair as she indulged in tears.

Ryan couldn't believe he had to do this or how much it tore him up inside. Ironic that now that he'd finally found a woman he wanted to spend time with, he was forced to let her go for her own good.

"I'll miss you," she said.

"That's hard to believe." His voice held a mirth she just could not muster. "Haley, I'm not the guy you need."

She pulled back, seeming to rally because she straightened her shoulders like a soldier at attention.

"So, is that how you do it? Give them a colossal orgasm, wine and a fine meal before shoving off?"

"Haley…it's not like that."

Her hands went to her hips. "How is it exactly? We going to meet up in NYC? You gonna call me from Africa on FaceTime?"

"Haley, I don't make promises I can't keep. I'm already assigned to my next gig."

"Got it. Thanks for breakfast. Very thoughtful." She extended her hand as if to shake goodbye.

He took her hand and kissed it. "I'm no good for you, you know?"

"Keep telling yourself that. Should make me easier to forget."

"I won't forget you, Haley." He turned and left the

room. She waited until she heard the door to the hallway click shut before she collapsed back into her chair.

"Well, I'll be doing everything I can to forget you,"
she whispered.

She had to. It was the only way to survive losing
the man with whom she had been stupid enough to
fall in love.

RYAN WONDERED IF he should just walk away and keep
walking. It was what he'd do in normal circumstances.
She was safe and their protective detail was en route.
She didn't need him and he surely did not need her.

But somehow he did.

Ryan hurried his steps, putting distance between
them. He had to get to the location that she'd decoded
from the thumb drive and as predicted there was time-
sensitive information there. Takashi's reason for moving the meet was now very clear.

In the lobby he lifted his phone and called Colonel Braiser, giving him the details and his course. His
friend and confidant Jorge Hernandez had assured him
that the leak had not come from their end. Ryan had to
go with that. Braiser said that the protective detail he'd
requested would make contact with Haley and escort
her away from Saratoga Springs.

As for his backup, they were en route and would be
redirected to the coordinates Ryan provided. In addi-
tion, they had a helicopter on standby ready for transport of the sample to the Center for Disease Control.
The bird was en route now and awaiting coordinates
for landing.

Haley had done her nation a great service. He planned to see she got the recognition she deserved in this case. But first he had to see about the vaccine and viral serum.

In the parking lot he paused to look back at the hotel.

What was happening here?

He lived by rules that had kept him from getting hurt. No attachments. The mission comes first.

"But does it?" Had he said that aloud?

Of course it did. Haley was sweet and smart and brave, but she wasn't coming with him on his next assignment. She shouldn't be here on this one.

Yet she'd been an asset. He knew of a few that preferred working in teams. Partners.

But not romantically involved. Not partners in the true sense. Is that what he wanted? Finish an assignment and come home to find Haley there asking, "How was your day, dear?"

"No," he muttered.

He wanted her in his bed every night and beside him when he wasn't bedding her.

"This is crazy."

He replayed Haley's goodbye in his mind. She'd seemed less shattered than furious. How had she thought this would end? More importantly, what did she want to happen between them?

It didn't matter what she wanted. She was going back to her life and he was returning to the mission. The colonel assured him that Haley would be protected.

Ryan had orders. But suddenly they didn't seem his whole world.

The problem was that he found everything about

Haley attractive. Not just the smell and feel of her. It was her smarts and her bravery. She'd been dealt a hard blow with the death of her sister. She didn't need to be involved with a man who might never come home. But beyond that, he had a mission. Everything else had to come second, even the woman he loved.

He would let her go now, while she was safe and he still had a mission that required his attention. Because if not for that mission he might just decide to keep her, make her believe he would survive the crazy risks he took and bring her along on his own personal adventure camp.

Ryan realized he was still standing before his vehicle after an unknown number of minutes. He snorted and lifted the fob. In less than thirty seconds, he was on his way.

HALEY SAT ALONE for a long while staring at the woods beyond the sunny little porch.

Ryan had left her behind. Was she a hindrance or was he protecting her? She thought of what he'd said in the woods about not being able to protect those men under his command. Since then he seemed to have taken every dangerous assignment possible and he worked alone. No risk of failing someone else. Survivor's guilt. Yes, that fit, but in his hurry to protect her, he was risking something she could not live without… Him.

She rose, knowing that she would not go back to adventure camp or back to her dad in Colonie or even back to Brooklyn and her consulting business.

She was going after Ryan. Perhaps he wouldn't need

her. But she was going, just the same. But first she had to steal a car. Haley yanked her hair into a ponytail and tucked the pistol he'd left her into the front of her bra. She wheeled it from the room to the bell stand. There she stowed the suitcase, collecting a claim check. Ryan would be furious, but Ryan was not here. She called the valet and ordered the GMC to be brought out front. Then she tucked the claim ticket in the tiny pocket of the tennis outfit and headed outside, where she handed over the ticket to one of the valets, got in the driver's door and drove away.

She programmed in the destination and, just like that, she was on her way north again, back to Lake George and the garnet mine that lay northwest of the lake.

Ryan was not going after that serum alone. She wasn't good backup, but perhaps her presence would be better than nothing. Besides, it could be worse. She could be preparing to fly down a zip line.

Chapter Twenty-One

Ryan discovered that the garnet mine was up a winding improved dirt road on the side of a mountain that offered zero chance of a helicopter landing. That meant he not only had to find and extract the biohazard, he had to transport it from this site. He bypassed the mine office and ignored the signs warning of private property, no trespassing and danger of blasting.

He had GPS coordinates and he continued on, through the open wire mesh gate and past the twelve-foot wire mesh perimeter fencing. The trees opened up to reveal a dirt parking lot that sparkled with the tiny glistening crystals of bloodred garnet. There were two work trailers, a nice variety of mud-spattered pickup trucks and heavy construction machinery. He recognized a bulldozer, backhoe and Bobcat. Before him was a thirty-foot rock wall with a crudely made road running along the base. A handful of men worked hydraulic jackhammers while the backhoe operator raked the tailings away from the cliff wall with the bucket. The pockets of garnet were obvious in the dark gray stone. They looked like circular patches of deep red glass. He knew enough about garnet to know it was used as an abrasive on sandpaper and emery boards, but imagined the industrial uses were many. He also imagined that the raw rock would be transported somewhere to be crushed and processed. From there it would be shipped anywhere in the world. And along with it, the biohazard, unless he could find it first.

According to Takashi's thumb drive, this was the first drop. From here it was destined for a production plant, the location of which was still unknown. The best way to find that plant was to allow the biohazard pickup and follow it to its destination.

But the colonel did not like to take chances. He wanted the toxin contained and in the hands of the CDC. Ryan could hardly disagree. Although waiting for backup might mean losing his chance. His realization was brought into sharp focus when a pickup truck drove past him, destined for who knew where. Hopefully not a drug manufacturing plant.

No time to wait, he decided and parked his vehicle with the others and checked his coordinates. This was the location. The trailers were the obvious place to store the package. Likely the office trailer had a refrigerator. Other possibilities were the garage, made from corrugated sheets of metal, or one of the trucks, many of which had long tool kits in their pickup beds.

A man stepped out of the office trailer. He wore a dirty hard hat, a frayed, insulated underwear shirt with dirty cuffs and ill-fitting jeans.

"Can I help you?" he asked.

Behind him, Ryan saw the window slide open and the barrel of a rifle aimed in his direction.

"Hey there!" he waved. "My kid is an absolute nut for rocks and minerals. You ever give tours up here?"

"No, mister. You're trespassing on private property."

Ryan was now standing in a position so that the shooter's line of sight was blocked by the man who confronted him.

"What about a sample then? I'll pay for it."

"I'm going to have to ask you to leave."

The man was covered in rock dust. He aimed a dirty hand in the direction of the gate. He was not, in Ryan's opinion, a member of Siming's Army or a mercenary. So he didn't kill him.

Ryan did throw him down the stairs, grabbing the hard hat from his head as he fell. Once inside, he threw the hard hat at the man by the window who was having trouble extracting his rifle barrel from the frame. Then he locked the trailer door.

Ryan had his pistol drawn and aimed at the guy's head. He made the right move, lifting his hands and letting the rifle fall to the bench seat beside him.

"Where is it?" Ryan asked.

"Where is what?"

"Up," Ryan said, using the pistol to motion him in the direction he wanted him to move.

The work trailer was open, showing a kitchenette and a padlocked closet.

"You got that key?" he asked.

The man nodded, sweating now as he continued toward the closet. He fumbled with his keys and released the lock.

"Open it," Ryan ordered. By now the worker outside would be up and either following him inside or running for help.

The guy opened the door. Ryan ordered him away and made a quick check. Then Ryan ordered him in and locked the door behind him.

Back in the kitchenette, Ryan opened the refrigerator and saw a neat red plastic cooler. He lifted it clear and set it carefully on the counter. Inside was a black leather case about five by seven by two inches that zipped closed. He opened it and stared at the two vials. Someone had secured the top of one with sealing wax, as one does a bottle of fine alcohol. The other vial just had a snap-on plastic cap. The vials were glass. The writing on the outside was Chinese or Korean or Japanese. He didn't know.

Now for the hard part: getting out of there.

The blast of automatic gunfire brought him to the ground. Beams of light shone through the multiple holes in the side of the trailer. Inside the closet, his captive screamed. Ryan hoped he was smart enough to get down.

The walls of the trailer were no match for the lead chewing through the exterior. And Ryan's handgun was no match for the weapons wielded by his foes. Two shooters, he judged from the directions of the gunfire and the angle of the bullets flying over his head. They circled the trailer, spraying it with bullets.

There were only two exits and both were on the

same side of the trailer. He now faced a terrible choice: destroy the samples or let them fall back into the hands of their enemies.

As the bullets chewed through the siding like termites though wet wood, he was glad that Haley was not here with him. But then her words echoed in his mind.

Maybe you are burying your guilt behind a revolving door of dangerous assignments.

She was right. And if he could figure out how to survive this assignment, he planned to tell her so.

HALEY LAY ON her belly on the ground beside the gate leading to the open-pit mine. Behind her, just past the view of anyone on the job site, was the GMC. She left the car close but out of sight, with the keys in the ignition.

She surveyed the scene, just as she had learned in her CPR class, looking for dangers, and saw nothing but a seemingly ordinary construction site.

The job site looked normal, with dump trucks picking up the tailings lifted into their enormous containers by a single-bucket evacuator. Men worked with jackhammers at the glittering pockets of garnet which were over ten feet in height and roughly circular.

But three men did not fit the scene. They were dressed in slacks and the sort of bulky jackets that could hide firearms.

They faced away from the job site and were stationed in lookout locations, but a shout brought them all running toward the office trailer.

Was Ryan here yet? Was he in there?

The answer came when they unloaded a torrent of automatic gunfire into the side of the flimsy structure.

She now had little doubt who was inside.

They were making such a racket that they did not hear her arrival as she headed for the construction vehicles.

She knew full well that the only way to get Ryan out was to get those men clear. And she wasn't doing that with the SUV or the handgun he'd left her. She needed some real horsepower. Something designed for ripping away earth and blowing through obstacles.

"Thanks, Dad," she whispered as she chose the familiar backhoe. It was perfect because it had a large bucket at the front and a small bucket on a stick and boom in the back. She climbed up the metal rungs and into the cab. Keys dangled in the ignition.

"Bingo." No reason to lock up vehicles that were already inside the locked perimeter. Just slowed down work. It was lazy, but it was commonplace, at least at the jobs she'd been on.

By the time the shooters realized she was heading for them, they had time only to scatter ahead of the backhoe. One of the pair fired and sparks flew off the steel bucket. They took cover behind the line of pickups and she just kept on coming.

Before she reached them, she lowered the bucket and angled the blade to the return-to-dig position and then plowed the trucks forward like dirt.

Her actions gave her time to swing the seat around and use the smaller bucket to tear a hole down the middle of the trailer.

Ryan appeared long enough to spot her, and grinned.

She was in Reverse when the gunfire cut through her tires. Didn't matter. She still managed to lift the bucket before her and ram it into the side of the trailer.

Ryan did not wait. He jumped into the raised bucket with a red Playmate cooler in one hand and his pistol in the other. Once he was on board, she lifted the bucket higher, giving him the advantage of height as she backed toward the gate. This, unfortunately, left her without the cover in the cab.

One of the men scrambled to open ground, lifting his weapon. With a flick of the lever she swung the stick left and the smaller bucket and boom forced him to dive into the dust. She maneuvered two levers now, retracting the boom and stick as she curled the bucket to give her some protection from the gunfire. Then she made for the gate.

From above her, Ryan returned fire. Sparks flew off the metal bucket, but she knew that even automatic weapons could not pierce the steel bucket.

The backhoe's windshield shattered as they reached the GMC. Ryan leaped out of the bucket and down the loader arm, reaching the SUV as she threw open the door to the backhoe and jumped to the ground.

When she threw herself into the passenger seat, he already had the SUV in gear and was flooring the gas, sending a rooster tail of dirt out behind them.

"Haley, are you crazy?" he yelled.

"Still think you don't need backup?" she asked.

He tore down the road. With the backhoe blocking

the only exit from the mining site, they might have a nice head start. But they needed to get to open ground.

"Check the samples. See if they are all right."

Gingerly, she opened the lid of the cooler, opened the case and examined the vials.

"Intact," she said and blew away a breath. Then she returned the case to the cooler and capped the lid. "I wonder what these things are exactly."

"I don't know, but I suspect the next person to handle them will be wearing a biohazard suit."

He concentrated on driving, taking the turns as fast as he could but still keeping them on the road. Haley buckled up and used the handle beside her door to help keep her in her seat as he raced around curves in the incline.

"You took a big chance coming back for me," he said.

"I sure did."

"Very brave," he added.

She looked at him with a tight-lipped expression that held both pity and aggravation. But she said nothing more.

He got them down the mountain road and handed her the phone.

"Call the last number as soon as you have a signal."

She held the phone out as if to coax the wireless connection. They'd nearly reached the highway when her satellite signal returned.

"Calling," she said.

"Put it on speaker."

The call connected and Ryan went through a series of words and responses that made no sense to her. But at completion, the man on the other end asked for their location.

"Route 28, from Indian River, northbound North Lake."

"Along the Hudson River," she added.

"We'll pull over when we see you coming."

"Roger that."

Haley held the phone out even though the caller had disconnected.

"How do you know that this guy will deliver the goods? Does he work for the Company?"

"Yes. He's solid. He'll bring this to Albany, where the colonel is waiting with a military plane to bring it to Washington, DC. Be there in a few hours if all goes to plan."

She looked at him and smiled. "How's your plan been going so far?"

He chuckled. His smile dropped away when he glanced in the rearview.

She used her side mirror and spotted another vehicle behind them. A moment later they veered onto Highway 28. Ryan cut left.

"Lake George is that way," she said.

"It's downhill. He needs a flat landing pad."

The SUV's engines revved as they sped off. The pickup truck hit the highway four hundred meters back.

The rhythmic thrum of the blades of a helicopter reached her.

"Hear that?" she asked.

"He's close." Ryan glance skyward.

Evergreens lined both sides of the highway with only

a narrow strip of tall grass flanking each side of the asphalt.

"Is it wide enough?"

"My man can land on a rooftop. And there's no power lines here. Question is, do we have time for him to land and take off again."

"I'll bring it to him. You give me cover," she said.

Ryan stared at her a moment and then nodded. He extended the flash drive. "Put that in the cooler."

She did.

Before them, an orange helicopter appeared. Ryan hit the brakes and turned them sideways, skidding to a halt. The chopper hovered and then descended. Haley jumped from the vehicle and ran, stooped over, through the clouds of burning rubber toward the helicopter, clutching the cooler. She ran as if her life depended on it when, in fact, she knew that many lives depended on it.

The chopper pilot opened his door and extended his hand for the cooler's handle, keeping one hand on the controls. In an instant he had a hold and was lifting off, door open. The pressure of the wind and the swirling dust caused Haley to drop to her knees and shield her face from the swirling debris.

The liftoff temporarily masked the sound of gunfire. But then she heard it. Automatic weapons repeating. She found herself alone on the highway with fifty yards between her and the SUV. Ryan was out of the vehicle and using the engine block as cover as he returned fire. It took her a moment to realize that his opponents were not firing at them. Their weapons were raised as they shot at the chopper, now rocketing toward the tree line to the right.

She could see the bullet holes appear on the tail section before the chopper swept over the treetops and out of sight.

The automatic weapons fell silent. Car doors slammed shut. An engine revved. By the time she jogged back to the SUV, their attackers were performing a neat three-point turn on the asphalt.

"They're leaving," she said in confusion.

He stood to watch them go.

"Look!" Haley pointed in the direction they had been heading at the line of five full-size SUVs barreling toward them.

His backup had arrived.

"More of Siming's Army?" she asked.

"Government plates," he said, pointing at the red, white and blue front tags.

Haley watched their pursuers speed away.

"Why didn't they kill us?" she asked.

"Killing us wasn't their mission. Protecting that cooler was."

"They failed," she said.

"Thank God. Now we'll have a chance of stopping them from using that toxin on innocent civilians."

The motorcade sped toward them and Ryan motioned them on. In a moment they were disappearing after the truck that had shot at the helicopter.

Haley watched after them for a moment and then turned back to Ryan.

"You did it," she said, her smile broadening as she

realized they had survived, would survive. Then she remembered that he'd be leaving her again and the smile died.

Ryan shielded his eyes with his hand as he looked at the clear blue sky.

"What are you looking for?" she asked, mimicking his stance as she followed the direction of his gaze.

"A fireball. I thought they hit the chopper early on."

"Me, too."

"If it crashes, we'll at least see black smoke."

Her jaw gaped as she scanned the impossibly blue sky. Minutes passed and there was nothing. Perhaps they been wrong and their attackers missed it.

Haley lowered her hand from above her eyes. "I think they missed it."

Ryan shook his head. "They didn't. But maybe they didn't take it down." He lowered his hand to his sides.

"What do we do now?"

Chapter Twenty-Two

Ryan pushed away from the exterior of the SUV that he had used as a backrest while looking for the chopper. He gripped his hands into fists as he tried to think of how to answer Haley's question.

He knew what would happen next. He'd endured many such partings, but up until now, he'd never cared. Now he faced a new dilemma. He did care, too much. Too much to involve her in his crazy choices and too much to let her go. But he'd have to do one or the other.

Their pursuers were gone and his mission complete, but there would be another mission and another. It was the life he had chosen and up until this moment he'd never questioned that decision.

Now he did.

He realized that he did not have to undertake such dangerous field assignments. It had been a choice, was a choice each time. He'd never hesitated until now.

Now he no longer wanted to die in some glorious and heroic fashion. The entire idea now seemed ludicrous. What he wanted instead was…Haley.

And a life of loving. He wanted what his parents had

shared. The magnificent gift of caring for and being cared for by another. He wanted to gain both the optimism required and commitment necessary to father a child.

He turned to face Haley.

"We need to talk," he said.

HALEY SWALLOWED AND then nodded her consent because she did not trust her voice.

Ryan left the vehicle and rounded to Haley's side, opening the door and offering his hand.

"I didn't want to do this here."

Her palms went wet. He was breaking up with her. She was certain. Why else would he look nervous for the first time since she'd met him?

It took all her courage. Somehow saying what was trapped inside her was harder than rock climbing or kayaking or cliff jumping. Because the risks here were so much higher. But she was not letting him go without telling him that she loved him because that was a risk she was not willing to take.

"Ryan, before you say anything, I want you to know that I understand now the importance of the work you do. And that I want to help, keep helping, I mean."

"You do?" he asked.

"I can't let you go yet."

"Why not?"

She drew a deep breath and held it for a moment, preparing for this metaphysical cliff jump.

"Because I've fallen in love with you."

His brows lifted halfway up his forehead as shock

registered on his face. Then he smiled. Was that the indulgent smile of a man about to let her down easily or a man truly pleased with her confession? She could not tell.

Her heart seemed to lodge in her throat like a jagged shard of glass.

"Haley, this isn't over yet. I have to get us clear and call in for orders."

It was worse than a rejection. It was a stall. She nodded her head, hoping he didn't see the trembling of her chin. Of course he didn't want to cut her loose on some highway in the mountains. She was brave enough for bullets but perhaps not brave enough to be rejected by the man she loved.

They drove to Indian Lake in silence. Once there, the satellite service returned and Ryan stepped out of the vehicle to make his call.

When he returned to the SUV his expression was grim.

"Chopper went down," he said. "They are sending a recovery team." He brushed his hand over his head, forward and back, then let his hand drop.

"Not you?"

He shook his head. "Recovery will be by air." He glanced toward the tree line. "The bird, cooler and thumb drive are missing with the pilot."

"That's bad."

"After all this, we might lose it all. Serum, virus and the intel."

Haley's brows lifted and she had a distinctively

guilty look on her face. She twisted her index finger in her opposite fist.

"Haley? What did you do?"

"Remember when I told you that this SUV has a special navigation system?"

"Yes."

"Well, I tried to explain but you said later. So, this is later, right?"

He nodded, clearly confused.

"The navigation system of this vehicle has a feature that could rip any CD placed into the player. That kind of storage system can also load MP3 files because it came with a USB port inside the center console. You could just plug in a memory stick to transfer files and it came with ten gigs of storage."

"How do you know this?"

"Major lawsuit in the tech industry. I pay attention."

"And why are you telling me this?"

"Because I used the MP3-GoGoMaker program in this GMC to copy the thumb drive into the navigation system."

"Those weren't music files," he said.

"So they are unreadable by that operating system. But they are still there."

"When did you do this?"

"When you were driving us. I tried to tell you." She fidgeted, tugging on her earlobe as she waited for his response.

"But you didn't. And you disobeyed orders."

"They weren't *my* orders." She smiled. "And you knew I was a hacker. It was too irresistible a temptation."

Ryan reached across her and pushed open her door. For just a moment she thought this was where he would leave her, after all he had the SUV and the intel stowed in the navigation system. He didn't need her.

"We best get this vehicle to my people. Why don't you drive?"

"Really?"

"Safer that way. I've got some phone calls to make."

He stepped out of the SUV, glancing back through the open door at her.

She rounded the vehicle and Ryan shut the door behind her.

Haley sat in the driver's seat and adjusted the seat, wheel, seat belt and mirrors. Her stomach twisted at the serious expression on Ryan's face as he climbed into the passenger seat and returned the phone to his pocket.

"Let's go."

Did that mean *let's get this over with*?

Chapter Twenty-Three

They drove south to the town of Half Moon, Haley still driving, Ryan still talking on the phone. One of his conversations surprised her. There were no code words or any other secret agent stuff. Just him asking to make an appointment and recording the time and date in the new phone.

"What was that about? Your injuries?"

"That's about seeing a shrink. Sorry, psychiatrist. I've seen her before but never bought into the fact that I might actually need to see her." He faced her.

"What changed your mind?" she asked.

He smiled at her, a warm, genuine smile that heated her skin and made her heart jump.

"You did."

She clasped her hands together at her heart. "Really? Ryan, I worked with a wonderful guy and, well, he's the reason I went into coding. Channeling, he called it, but after all this and what my dad said, I think I have some more work to do as well because I miss getting out there. Not the bullets part, though."

He nodded at that. "The bullets seem to be part of

my problem. My CO has referred me to a counselor. I can accept what was obvious to you and to my CO. I want to talk to someone about my time in the military."

She gripped his hands. "Oh, Ryan, really?"

He laughed. "Really." He lifted his brow. "Maybe we can get a group discount."

She laughed at that, the relief and the unexpected arrival on the other side of danger filling her with a giddy elation. Driving swiftly along in traffic with the pavement humming beneath the tires just felt right. Heading home, safe.

"That's our exit," said Ryan, pointing.

Haley made the turn onto the ramp at Half Moon.

Every time she drove down the Northway with her dad he'd mention that this place had been named for the Dutch ship the *Halve Maen*, that sailed up the Hudson River in 1609, captained by an Englishman, Henry Hudson, in the employment of the Dutch Republic.

Here she finally met Colonel Charles Braiser, who looked more like the owner of the riverside cabin where they stopped than a colonel. His short military-style cut was secreted under a ball cap and his attire was definitely civilian. The man appeared to be in his midforties and fit enough to run a 5K on demand.

He shook her hand and said words she never expected to hear.

"Thank you for your service to your country, Miss Nobel."

His hand slipped away and she managed to close her gaping mouth.

The SUV was transferred to a group of fierce, frightening-looking men who appeared as if they would be as comfortable diving headfirst out of an airplane as guarding the intelligence Ryan delivered.

Once the men were away, the colonel turned to Ryan. "We have a vehicle waiting. Would you like me to have Miss Nobel returned home?"

Haley held her breath.

Ryan shook his head. "That won't be necessary."

The colonel did a poor job hiding his surprise.

"Very well, then. Debrief tomorrow."

Ryan gave a crisp salute and then accepted the keys from the colonel. A touch of the fob and a sweet blue Mustang flashed its lights at them.

It was unfortunate that her first ride in a muscle car would be her last one with Ryan. Those tears threatened again, but she cleared her throat and let herself into the passenger side.

She didn't ask why he'd dumped her at the hotel or where he was dropping her. She really didn't care. Her entire being was fixed on getting through this without weeping.

When he exited at Colonie, she was not surprised. He was dropping her at her father's place then. But he was a smart man. He wouldn't break up with her until they were parked in the driveway.

Ryan cut the engine and cleared his throat. Haley braced herself.

He straightened his shoulders as if preparing for battle and muttered "Okay" under his breath. He slipped out from behind the wheel of the sports car and rounded the hood. She had the door open when he reached her but allowed him to assist her up. Man, these Mustangs rode low to the pavement.

"Did you know that my orders included leaving you behind?" he asked.

"They did?"

"Yes. I was authorized to use deadly force against anyone who interfered with or impeded my mission."

License to kill, she realized. How many times had she slowed him down? But she'd helped him, too. More than once.

"I never wanted to let you go until, well, until I knew my chances were poor. I couldn't risk your life again."

"That's why you left me?"

He nodded.

"But I could have helped you! I *did* help you. And leaving me was not best for your mission."

"No, it wasn't."

"So why did you do that?"

He pressed his lips together. "Don't you know?"

She shook her head.

"Because it was best for you."

She stepped closer, hope flickering in her hammering heart.

"I've fallen in love with you, Haley. You are an amazing, brave and resourceful woman."

"Ryan?"

"I don't want to cut you loose. I want to wake up to see you in my bed every morning."

"You do?" she squeaked.

"What do you think about that, Haley?"

In answer she leaped into his arms and kissed him with all the joy and promise she had kept locked so tightly in her heart.

When they finally came up for air, he was laughing and she was crying.

"I want to meet your parents," he said.

"Now?"

"As soon as possible."

"To thank them?" she asked, hoping she had guessed wrong.

"To ask their permission to marry their daughter. Their wonderful, fearless daughter."

Haley staggered back a step. He tethered her with one hand and then yanked until she fell flush against him.

"I…I…think that could be arranged. But maybe we should have dinner a time or two first."

"If you think that's best."

"So they'll know we're serious."

He chuckled. "Oh, we're serious all right."

He threaded his fingers into her hair and kissed her again. When she came up for air, she saw a strange, un-familiar look on his face, almost wistful.

"What?" she asked as his brow swept low over dark eyes.

"My mom would have loved you."

She made an involuntary sound in her throat at the sweetness of that sentiment.

"I'm sure I would have loved her, too."

He clasped her hand and brought it to his mouth, brushing the lightest kiss across her knuckles.

"I have a confession to make," she said.

His smile faded as he braced for bad news.

"The FBI has tried to recruit me. Several times, in fact. But I make more money as a private contractor."

"You are too good for the FBI."

"You have no idea how good I am."

"Oh, I disagree with you on that one."

"Maybe I should consider the Company and the Bureau. Set up a bidding war between them."

"Maybe," he said and laughed. His arm snaked around her waist and he squeezed. "It will be nice to have a brilliant fiancée who is in high demand."

"And to have a secret agent saving the world while taking only necessary risks. Right?"

He laughed. "That sounds wise…for a married man."

Haley beamed up at him. "Are we really getting married?" she asked.

"Appears that way."

"Do we plan on a honeymoon?" she asked.

"That would be nice. Why? Do you have a spot picked out?" he asked.

"Costa Rica."

He nodded, finding the spot appealing and surprising, just like his soon-to-be fiancée.

"Why there?"

"Because they have rainforests and a zip-line tour that runs right through them."

He laughed. "A zip line? Really?"

She looped her hands around his neck.

"Then we have to find a cliff jump."

"Sounds exciting."

"Yeah. I'm ready for some excitement."

"These last few days weren't exciting enough?"

"More like terrifying. But also just the first of many, many adventures together."

* * * * *

COMING NEXT MONTH FROM

HARLEQUIN®

INTRIGUE

Available July 16, 2019

#1869 IRON WILL
Cardwell Ranch: Montana Legacy • by B.J. Daniels
Hank Savage is certain his girlfriend was murdered, so he hires private investigator Frankie Brewster to pretend to be his lover and help him find the killer. Before long, they are in over their heads...and head over heels.

#1870 THE STRANGER NEXT DOOR
A Winchester, Tennessee Thriller • by Debra Webb
After spending eight years in jail for a crime she didn't commit, Cecelia Winters is eager to find out who really killed her father, a religious fanatic and doomsday prepper. In order to discover the truth, she must work with Deacon Ross, a man who is certain Cecelia killed his mentor and partner.

#1871 SECURITY RISK
The Risk Series: A Bree and Tanner Thriller • by Janie Crouch
A few months ago, Tanner Dempsey saved Bree Daniels, but suddenly they find themselves back in danger when Tanner's past comes back to haunt the couple. Will the pair be able to stop the criminal before it's too late?

#1872 ADIRONDACK ATTACK
Protectors at Heart • by Jenna Kernan
When Detective Dalton Stevens follows his estranged wife, Erin, to the Adirondack Mountains in an effort to win her back, neither of them expects to become embroiled in international intrigue. Then they are charged with delivering classified information to Homeland Security.

#1873 PERSONAL PROTECTION
by Julie Miller
Ivan Mostek knows two things: someone wants him dead and a member of his inner circle is betraying him. With undercover cop Carly Valentine by his side, can he discover the identity of the traitor before it's too late?

#1874 NEW ORLEANS NOIR
by Joanna Wayne
Helena Cosworth is back in New Orleans to sell her grandmother's house. Suddenly, she is a serial killer's next target, and she is forced to turn to Detective Hunter Bergeron, a man she once loved and lost, for help. Together, will they be able to stop the elusive French Kiss Killer?

YOU CAN FIND MORE INFORMATION ON UPCOMING HARLEQUIN® TITLES, FREE EXCERPTS AND MORE AT WWW.HARLEQUIN.COM.

HICNM0719

Get 4 FREE REWARDS!

We'll send you 2 FREE Books plus 2 FREE Mystery Gifts.

Harlequin Intrigue® books feature heroes and heroines that confront and survive danger while finding themselves irresistibly drawn to one another.

FREE Value Over **$20**

It wasn't long before they were arriving at the ranch. He
grabbed her overnight bag, and they walked inside.

"We both need to get a few hours' sleep," he said. "I'll
take the couch and you can have the bed."

She walked toward the bedroom but turned at the
door. "Come with me. Just to sleep together like before."
Those big green eyes studied him as she reached her hand
out toward him.

There was nothing he wanted more than to curl up
with her in his bed. But with his anger and frustration so
close to the surface, he couldn't discount the fact that he
might wake up swinging. The thought of Bree being the
recipient of his night terrors made him break out into a
cold sweat.

"Never mind," she said quickly, misreading his hesitation,
hand falling back to her side. "You don't have to."

Damn it, he'd rather never sleep again than see that wounded look in her eyes from something he'd done.

He stepped toward her. "I want to. Trust me, there's nothing I want more. But…I just don't want to take a chance on waking you up if I get called back in to Risk Peak early." That was at least a partial truth.

The haunted look fell away from her eyes, and a shy smile broke on her face. "I don't mind. I'll take a shorter amount of sleep if it means I get to sleep next to you."

He would have given her anything in the world to keep that sweet smile on her face. He took her hand, and they walked into the bedroom together.

They took turns changing into sleep clothes in the bathroom, then got into the bed together. The act was so innocent and yet so intimate.

Tanner rolled over onto his side and pulled Bree's back against his front. He breathed in the sweet scent of her hair as her head rested in the crook of his elbow. His other arm wrapped loosely around her waist.

She was out within minutes, her smaller body relaxing against him, trusting him to shelter and protect her while she slept. Tanner wouldn't betray that trust, even if that meant protecting her against himself.

Besides, sleeping was overrated when he could be awake and feeling every curve that had been haunting his dreams for months pressed against him.

Definitely worth it.

Don't miss
Security Risk *by Janie Crouch,*
available August 2019 wherever
Harlequin® Intrigue books and ebooks are sold.

www.Harlequin.com

HIEXP0719

"You've been avoiding me," Eden added, and she set the grocery
bags on the small kitchen counter.

"I have," he admitted, and he wanted to wince. This was the
problem with crossing a line with a friend. He wasn't used to putting
on mouth filters when it came to Eden. "I wanted to give us both
some time."

Her eyebrow came up, and she huffed before she mumbled some
frustrated profanity under her breath.

"See?" he snapped, as if that proved all the arguments going on in
his head. "We're uncomfortable with each other, and it's all because
of the kiss that shouldn't have happened."

She stared at him a moment, caught on to a handful of his shirt
and yanked him to her. She kissed him. Hard.

Nico felt his body jolt, an involuntary reaction that nearly made
him dive in for more. After all, good kisses should be deep and
involve some tongue. It was like stripping off a layer of clothes or
going to the next level. But those were places that Nico stopped
himself from going. Before their tongues could get involved, he

stepped back from her, and she let go of him, her grip melting off his shirt.

He felt the loss right away when her mouth was no longer on his. The loss and the realization that Eden was a real, live, breathing woman. An attractive one with breasts, legs and everything.

Oh man.

He didn't want to realize that. He wanted his friend. And he wanted that friendship almost as much as he wanted to French-kiss her.

"Now we can also be uncomfortable because of that kiss I just gave you," she said, as if that proved whatever point she'd been trying to make. It proved nothing. Well, nothing that should be proved anyway.

Nico stared at her. "Eden, you're playing with a thousand gallons of fire," he warned her—after he'd caught his breath.

"I know, and I'm going to be honest about that. In fact, I'm going to insist we be honest with each other so that we don't ruin our friendship."

That was very confusing, and Nico wondered if this was some kind of trick. Except Eden wasn't a trick-playing kind of person. "What the heck do you mean by that?"

Her gaze stayed level with his. "It means if you want to kiss me, you should. If you don't want to kiss me again, then don't."

He was still confused. About what she was saying anyway. Nico was reasonably sure that the wanting-to-kiss-her part was highly charged right now.

"I just don't want you to avoid me because you're struggling with this possible curveball that's been tossed into our friendship," Eden went on. "That kiss makes us even," she added with a firm nod.

Don't miss
Sweet Summer Sunset *by Delores Fossen,*
available July 2019 wherever HQN books
and ebooks are sold.

www.Harlequin.com